MAGICAL EYES

DAWN OF THE SAND

2022

JESSICA D'AGOSTINI

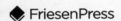

FriesenPress

Suite 300 - 990 Fort St
Victoria, BC, V8V 3K2
Canada

www.friesenpress.com

Copyright © 2017 by Jessica D'Agostini
First Edition — 2017

ISBN
978-1-4602-9719-3 (Hardcover)
978-1-4602-9720-9 (Paperback)
978-1-4602-9721-6 (eBook)

1. JUVENILE FICTION, FANTASY & MAGIC

Distributed to the trade by The Ingram Book Company

DEDICATION

To my sweet and charming daughter,
who took me back to a wonderful world of fantasies.

TABLE OF CONTENTS

MAGICAL EYES

DAWN OF THE SAND

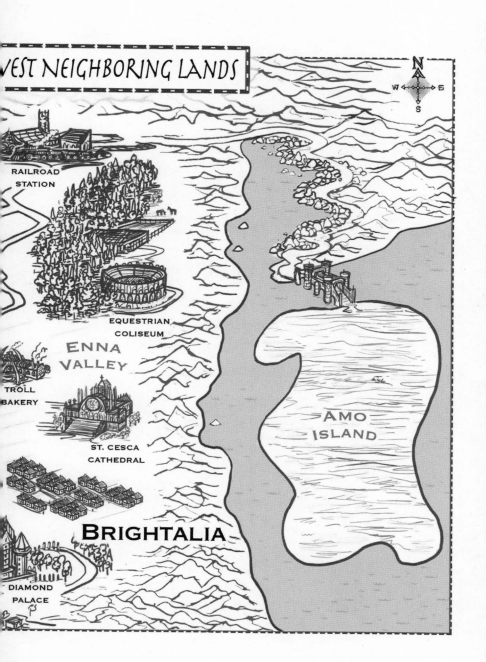

CHAPTER ONE

For a thousand years, a kingdom lived in terror under a dark wizard with a magical book. Nobody saw the mysterious book again; they presumed it had been destroyed. But the legacy of that evil ruler was never forgotten, and fear remained in the village. After the sorcerer was poisoned by one of his guards, all magic was banned forever at the royal palace—even during special events like the one all the townspeople were about to witness.

It happened on a Sunday morning. King Alessio and Queen Constanza were more than ready for the celebration. They both hoped for a perfect day, which meant no magic of any sort or spells offered by the master wizards. The royal couple had made every notable attempt to have a normal life.

The queen oversaw the rehearsal of the entire ceremony six times. The king practiced his speech nine times. And they both reviewed every agenda twice. And a third time. And just in case, a fourth time. Not an easy task considering their busy schedules. They were confident that nothing had been overlooked.

Yellow rays brightened Enna Valley. Villagers opened the windows and doors of their shops. Not a single cloud covered the blue sky. Cypress trees danced to the rhythm of a pleasant song.

"Where is that music coming from?" an artisan asked, inching along Main Street. He carried a basket full of handcrafted straw hats.

"Don't you know? It's Presentation Day!" responded a small boy as he struggled among the multitude of adults.

"Move, Enzo!" said his mom, rushing in. Dressed in black, the woman covered her face with a veil. "I stood in line a whole morning under the sun to get a royal pass. We can't afford to be late."

Flowers decorated the entire village, softening the massive architecture of the Brightalia Kingdom. Even gargoyles had lavender stuffed into their monstrous mouths. Tilted or straight, every statue had a laurel wreath on its head. And like candy canes, there were red ribbons wrapped around the carved white columns of Piano Plaza.

Diamond Palace sat atop a green hill overlooking the valley. It was the most impressive building in town. Its corner towers were totally covered in stained glass and flashed radiant colors in the sunlight. The same dazzling rays that made the day look perfect.

Peasants and villagers had already started gathering at Piano Plaza, right in front of the royal residence. The crowd chatted. There was excitement in their voices. Children played around the plaza. The Diamond Presentation was about to begin. A new princess had been born.

"Here they come!" said Enzo, jumping up and down. He was an unusual boy, with the outline of a fish on his left cheek.

"I wish your dad was here," mumbled his mom. After the

unexpected murder of her husband, Julia had no choice but to flee from the neighboring kingdom of Castella. Now living in hiding, the new widow and refugee carried the heavy burden of supporting her poor son. "Let's keep walking to the front," added Julia as a tear rolled down her wrinkled face. Not as old as she looked, the woman was only in her late forties. Many blamed her lung disease for her prematurely aged appearance. Even her own son had teased her about getting old too soon.

Guards lined up along the palace's entrance, and the band began playing at the veranda. The blare of the trumpets was majestic.

The double doors of the main balcony opened up, revealing the royal family of Brightalia.

A hush descended over the multitude. All heads turned toward the magnificent palace.

Alessio XIV carried his baby girl with deep affection. Next to him, Queen Constanza proudly stood, holding their son's hand. Both King Alessio and Queen Constanza shimmered with their royal crowns. They flashed their most jubilant smiles. Prince Drago also grinned from ear to ear.

King Alessio stepped forward and said in a tender voice, "All these people are here to see you." He gently squeezed the baby in his arms. The king wore a long coat with matching midnight blue trousers. His ruffled white shirt and thick belt were perfectly aligned along his round belly. The baby princess had an impeccable white flowing dress. The long delicate gown rippled in the soft breeze.

Queen Constanza also advanced to the front of the balcony. Her fine cloak trailed behind her, giving everybody an exquisite feel to the moment. The elegant off-white gown was embroidered in gold and silver. The blue diamond on the queen's necklace was the highlight of her attire; not to underestimate her slim figure. Prince Drago, who kept his pace next to his mom, wore a black ceremonial outfit.

As the royal family reached the front of the balcony, drums began to beat. With great pride, King Alessio presented his daughter, raising her up into the air. Queen Constanza royally saluted her citizens. Prince Drago, with a poker smile, also greeted the multitude. But it was Princess Martina who captured everybody's attention. She opened her eyes and looked at the crowd. Her dazzling eyes glittered with the sun, a violet color never seen before. Her hair was shiny black, and her rosy cheeks enhanced her soft white skin. Everybody was stunned. It was a special moment in the history of the Brightalia Kingdom.

"Beautiful Martina!" shouted Enzo.

"Don't scream, son!" whispered Julia, pulling the boy by the hand. She straightened Enzo's shirt, getting ready to climb up the grassy hill. She had carefully read the instructions in her ceremonial pass. "Let's get in line!"

Inside the palace, royal councilors and ambassadors had already lined up to bow and curtsy to the new member of the royal family. Later, selected villagers and farmers were to join the procession to greet the baby princess.

As Enzo and his mom got close to the crystal bassinet, the little boy placed a small present at the feet of the baby. "This is all I have to give you," muttered Enzo, looking at Martina.

"Dear! This wooden box might seem empty, but it's actually full of good wishes," said Julia in a kind voice.

"Thank you for the thoughtful gift," said King Alessio.

Julia lowered her head. "Oh! Your Majesty, I needed to be here today. My husband passed away, and I was left with nothing. Please help me. I'm in desperate need of a job to feed my son." She rested her arms on Enzo's shoulders.

"I am sure we can assist you, madam. Bring your alms request next week." King Alessio smiled at the three-year-old boy, ruffling his hair affectionately.

"Father, hurry up!" jumped in Prince Drago, rolling his eyes. He gave Enzo a stern look.

Enzo turned his head away, pretending to be gazing at the banquet buffet, which in fact, was unquestionably more appealing than the prince. He forced himself to remain quiet just as his mother had instructed.

"I will see what the Royal Council can find for you," added King Alessio. Then he raised his hand politely, showing Julia and her son the villagers' area in the stylish ballroom.

As the young boy and his mother reached a corner table at the back of the great hall, a loud screech sounded. The noise quickly filtered inside the ceremony room as if a firecracker had crashed to the floor. The precocious boy darted to a window. He spotted a white bird flying toward the palace. It flapped its long broad wings a few times and then glided over the plaza. Chaos grew among the throng. Some people ran to adjacent streets. Others crawled along the grass to find refuge behind the stone benches or under the closest maple tree, while some stood like mummies as their jaws dropped.

Enzo poked his head out of the window. "It's a white fish eagle!" screamed the boy eagerly. He clambered up to the stone sill.

"Enzo, *nooo!*" yelped Julia, coughing. Her voice trembled with fear. She took several deep breaths, trying to get some air into her lungs as she rushed behind her son.

The large fowl squealed, picking up speed. It brushed the balcony with its hooked bill, letting out another wail.

Enzo covered his ears, deaf from the loud cry. As much as he tried, he could not keep his balance. The boy toppled backward, falling down to the floor. "Ouch!" Enzo scooted to his mom, his eyes fixed on the fluffy feathered creature.

King Alessio raced to the window. His heart jumped to his throat as though he had just crossed the finish line of a fifty-meter dash. He narrowed his eyes at the bird. Enzo was correct: a white fish eagle. The bird was unusually large—almost the size of a dragon.

"What's going on?" mumbled the king between his teeth.

Julia helped Enzo to his feet. "Don't you ever do that again! You know you could have fallen to—"

"Are you okay, boy?" interrupted King Alessio.

"Super-duper, Your Majesty!"

And there was no time to say another word. The white eagle thrashed inside the ballroom. It tripped over two champagne fountains. Bubbles and glass covered the wood floor. Guests fled, pushing each other out of the way to hide, horror-stricken looks on their faces.

The fish eagle headed toward the baby. It dug its claws into the bassinet and settled for a moment. Then, the imposing bird extended its wings and emitted a harsh squawk causing some of the stained glass in the tall windows to break. Finally, it flew back out, soaring up into the open air.

King Alessio paused for a moment, forcing his anxiety down. He cleared his throat loudly. Then he turned back to the startled guests. "Everything is fine. It was an ordinary annoying bird. It's hard to teach animals proper manners," said the king, trying for a fake laugh.

The white eagle kept circling around the palace, five times according to Enzo. Straight away, the crystal cradle twinkled in the ballroom. A violet light gleamed up to the ceiling. After a second or two, the bassinet slowly rose into the air, a few inches off the ground. It was better than watching a neat performance of a levitation act. It floated toward an open fire. The flames began to vanish rather quickly. They changed from vivid red to a cream color, and it did not take long for the entire flames to be gone. A stream of smoke lingered in the grand ballroom, and only sand remained at the hearth.

King Alessio and Queen Constanza exchanged astonished looks. "Sand?" they whispered at the same time.

The queen could barely speak. "What's happening?" She pressed her hands against her chest. A rush of panic swept over her. She was paralyzed in fear.

A good omen for the baby, I hope! thought King Alessio with a tense face. He was not able to articulate even one word. As much as he tried, this time he could not manage to hide his nervousness.

Still suspended in midair, the bassinet swayed to the center of the room. Palace visitors moved in all different directions, avoiding contact with the floating cradle. At last, it made a safe, steady landing on the dance floor. The air cleared completely as if a vacuum had sucked up all the smoke.

"It is time to take you to the nursery," said Queen Constanza, grabbing the newborn baby from the bassinet. Queen Constanza smiled at the guests, and holding Martina tight in her arms, she led the way out of the ballroom.

Councilors clustered around the bassinet. The bemused villagers looked at one another. Enzo, who also wanted to inspect the cradle, felt a strong grip. Julia had crushed his small fingers.

"Sorcery," said one of the dignitaries. "I knew it when I saw her piercing eyes."

A complete hush filled the room. Everybody resembled a perfect statue, except they did not have laurel wreaths on their heads. But King Alessio took a deep breath and immediately signaled the musicians to resume playing.

It took some more gossip time for the posh nobles to start

enjoying the celebration. Some councilors went on the dance floor while many gathered around the exquisite buffet. Enzo maneuvered around the hors d'œuvres tables, spotting a tasty pastry. He grabbed a plate and filled it with cheese canapés. Doing a lively jig, he scampered across the room until he found his corner table. The same age as Prince Drago, but slightly shorter, the young peasant placed his pile of yellow canapés in front of him. His mouth watered as he caught a whiff of the melted cheese. When the boy got ready to take the first bite, the candlelights went out. Diamond Palace was in total darkness.

"She's a witch!" A voice echoed off the walls of the grand ballroom.

CHAPTER TWO

At Enna Valley, some sporadic rumors still circulated about Martina's Presentation despite all the years. In fact, it became remembered as Eagle Sunday. At Diamond Palace, the event was a deleted scene of the past. Nobody could reference or mention the celebration. It was a royal order from Queen Constanza. She was the primary champion for keeping magic away from the palace. The crystal bassinet was confined to the black walls of a room far away at the end of the stables. Well, not before the master wizards carefully examined the entire bassinet to realize that it was just an ordinary baby cradle. Maybe they were searching in the wrong place. Or maybe they did not look hard enough. One thing was certain, almost eight years had gone by and life had been as normal as the queen wished, at least to her eyes.

As for the princess, she was shut out from the outside world. The villagers never saw her again. She stayed hidden. Martina learned to accept that she could not leave the palace. Yet opposite to what many believed, she had turned into a charming girl. She did not look like a witch at all. And who had a vile temper? Wrong guess to think about Martina. She displayed a caring and positive attitude all the time. She enjoyed playing by herself, and she also loved to be with her brother. Martina and Drago were three years apart, but their differences in character spread over distant decades. As little kids, the two siblings shared many nice memories together. They were best friends. But as they grew up, Drago's strong personality started taking them apart.

"Can I play?" said the princess, sitting on a bench. Martina enjoyed spending time at the West Yard of the palace.

"Sure! After you grow a couple of more inches!" responded Drago, passing by the bench. The prince had invited some children of courtiers to play with him that afternoon.

Martina stood and followed closely behind Drago. "I might not be as tall as you are, but I'm a quick runner."

"Huh!" Prince Drago turned and faced Martina. "It's not about racing fast. It's about strength and power and all the attributes that only boys have. A girl can't play Bladeking."

Martina sighed. "I have my own wooden sword, and I've been practicing."

"Oh yeah! With whom?" But Drago thought for a moment and quickly realized that he might need some help. Then he grabbed Martina's hand and tossed her a whistle. "Here! Now you're officially in the game." He winked at her.

"Fine. I'll be the referee," said Martina in a low voice. She was not an expert, but she knew some of the rules, at least the basic ones. She was surely aware that a player stepping out of bounds, losing his sword or striking an opponent in the back resulted in the opposing team gaining five points as penalty.

"Boys, come this way," said Drago, waving his hand. He reached a small shed near one corner of the field. He started pulling out his wooden swords.

"I have a better idea! Why don't we play archery instead?"

suggested Rocco, adjusting his thick glasses.

"I'm in for archery!" agreed Loretto, the boy with a peculiar look. Drago called him "Stick". It was easy to guess why. He was so thin and tall that he mirrored a stick insect.

"Sounds good to me too. Last time we played sword fighting." Mattean kept track of everything, even a mosquito passing by.

"And we're only five. We'll need one more fighter for Bladeking," finished Lummy, Drago's best pal.

"Not today! We'll play Bladeking," said Drago determined to play his game. "I got the extra player." He turned toward the stables and let out a couple of whistles. "You'll see."

One of the stall helpers came running. He wore a white grubby shirt rolled up to his elbows, khaki shorts with a few holes and a pair of not-so-polished old boots. "Hi guys," said Enzo, raising one hand.

"This is Fish-face." Drago pursed his mouth in a wide smirk.

The group burst into peals of laughter at the appearance of the poor villager.

"Stop it, guys!" Martina said fiercely. "Why don't you get your weapons?"

Still chuckling, Drago pulled out a new sword from a sheath. "My new baby."

"Whoah! You got a KIL500!" said Lummy.

"Yeah!" nodded Drago, raising an eyebrow. He handed Lummy his new finely crafted sword.

"Cool! It's so light and neat to wield." The spiky hair boy admired the top-notch sword, making some flourish movements. The rest of the boys gathered around Lummy, except for Enzo who had to tiptoe to peer over Lummy's shoulder.

"Cherrywood. Awesome!" added Mattean.

"Careful!" Prince Drago smiled and entered the shed to pick up the leather armors. "Here guys! Put on your vests." He also pulled out some wrist and leg guards.

After they all took a close look at the five-star sword, they put on their body armor and guards. Drago's friends got to pick their swords. Of course, none was like the new KIL500. Enzo was handed a KIL009, one of the first models. It was old and shorter than the rest of the swords. Yet it looked perfect to him. He had some Bladeking knowledge from playing street games with broomsticks.

"I'll be the captain for my team!" Drago raised his arm.

"I'll be the other captain," Lummy said quickly.

Drago called out the names of his teammates. "Rocco and Mattean. You're my fighters." He needed to be the first one. He knew which of his friends were good at fencing. "I must win!" Drago whispered as he handed out green headbands to Lummy. "We'll be the Blue Vipers."

"Sure! We'll take green. The Green Lizards are ready," said Lummy, tightening his band.

"Lummy, Fish-face and Loretto! Let's go Green Lizards!" added Loretto, encouraging his teammates.

Drago's team also wrapped their blue headbands around their foreheads. They all moved to the center of the field to prepare their gold dohkets or round flat disks. Plus or minus the size of a pancake, all dohkets were made out of clay, and then painted in gold. The kingdom's coat of arms was stamped on both sides of the disk. Now, it was the task of each player to insert a dohket into the clear pocket of his armor.

Martina helped some of the boys. "Don't do it like Mattean. The pocket goes to the front."

"Had to be Professor Wit," giggled Drago.

"Okay, okay! I was thinking about my electromagnetic wave project," said Mattean in a brisk voice. He removed his armor, turned it around, and shoved it over his big head properly.

He saw how Enzo paid close attention to avoid making this same mistake.

"Let it slide by itself. You don't want to break the dohket now," advised Martina. She watched Lummy, putting in place his gold target. The princess was on top of every detail.

"Thank you, Martina," smiled Lummy, centering his disk.

Aiming for the dohket was the main purpose of the popular game. If a player struck with his sword the thin disk of an opponent breaking it, that warrior would gain ten points for his team, and the opponent fighter would have to leave the game. Bladeking ended when a team eliminated all members of the opposing group, receiving an additional twenty points. The team with the highest score won the combat.

Martina stood in the middle of the field waiting for the Blue Vipers and the Green Lizards to take their spots at each end. The captains shook hands before positioning behind their teammates.

Martina looked to both sides. "You can draw your swords," she declared with a firm voice. Then she pressed the white whistle firmly between her lips and blasted the start of the game, running to the edge of the field.

Both warrior teams charged to the center with determined looks to win the match. It was a one-on-one battle, at first.

Prince Drago spread his legs apart as he sparred. "Ready, Stick?" He watched his opponent while holding his weapon up. Loretto moved into attack and launched his first strike.

Drago quickly parried the swinging blow. "You missed your hit!" celebrated the prince. He immediately swung the flat of his sword and sent a strike. Loretto was fast, and Drago received his first block.

"Take this one!" Loretto raised his weapon, but Drago slammed it aside before the boy could attack. The green warrior managed to balance his sword. With every swipe, the prince sent Loretto to the end of the field, almost outside to get the first five points for his team.

But the game was interrupted by the referee's whistle before Loretto set a foot out of bounds. "Blue fighter disarmed!" Lummy twisted Rocco's blade, sending it spinning into the air. "Five points go to the Green Lizards."

The green team cheered.

"Guys! You need to focus. Turn on your brains and power up your muscles!" instructed Drago. He and his teammates clustered together to try to come up with a strategy.

"Position and arm yourself!" shouted Martina. The whistle blower signaled the restart of the action. She watched closely all the warrior's movements, attempting to show Drago her advanced Bladeking knowledge.

Lummy had improved his engagement skills. Almost every afternoon, he practiced by slashing oak tree branches when walking home from school. This time, he got ready to make some strategic attacks. He hurled himself at Rocco, but he deflected it without difficulty. They engaged in an intense fight. Sweat dripped down to the ground. Lummy avoided a blow with a single twist. He then sidestepped, allowing the opening for a clear shot. And he took it. The point of Lummy's sword bashed straight at the dohket of the blue player, breaking his gold target. "Gotcha Rocco!" he whooped.

"After vigorous moves, Rocco is out, and the Green Lizards increase their score up to fifteen. Are the Blue Vipers awake? They do not seem to be too alert today. Well, that can happen. Even the best teams have bad days," narrated Martina.

"Shut up, Martina. I didn't ask you to be a commentator!" said Drago, raising his voice.

"Chill, my friend," responded Lummy. "It's just a game. Losing or winning, you'll still get your juice after the battle."

"Prince Drago never loses." His ears turned pink. He gripped his sword tightly and screamed, "Whistle!"

The battle resumed. Drago kept pressing Mattean to play tough. He knew they could not afford any silly mistakes. An error could cost them the game. He soon forgot his training practices and went with his natural aggressive instincts, trying to intimidate his opponent. He skittered rapidly and pointed his weapon straight at Enzo. With his arms outstretched, Drago used all his strength for his next attack. He made a surprise lunge at Enzo, who maneuvered to repel the difficult blow. Drago turned into a continuous whap machine. Enzo struggled, but deflected most of the blows while striving for some counterattacks. But Drago was quick and dodged extremely well. He overpowered Enzo and dominated the fight. At last, Enzo tripped over some rocks. But there was a new interruption.

"Blue fighter out of bounds. Five points goes to the Green Lizards," said Martina with a whistle blast.

"Mattean! Are you dancing or fighting?" screamed Drago, retracting his blade away from Enzo. The tip of his sword was an inch or two from Enzo's dohket. Drago's face was as red as a ripe tomato. "You won't escape next time. You'll see what it is to fight a prince!"

"Hey, I'm battling two guys at the same time," shouted back Mattean. "You should thank me instead!"

Enzo sighed. He needed the quick break. The street fights had helped, but no one was as hectoring as Drago. He ran to the other side of the field at the sound of the whistle, avoiding the prince.

After a couple of minutes, two more players were out of the match. Concise and clear, the referee announced, "Green warrior out. Blue fighter also hit. Each team gets awarded ten points." The princess could not resist and whispered, "The blue team captain chased and knocked over Fish-face. His golden disk was smashed into pieces. I'm impressed! He was not a bad fighter. At last, the Blue Vipers received their first ten points. Thanks go to my brother. Captain Lummy also demonstrated his skills by taking Mattean out of combat. Now it is only up to the strong fighter Drago to defend the blue honor. The Green Lizards outmatch their opponent team with two warriors in the battlefield and lead the game with thirty points. In my opinion, they have a great chance of winning. No offense to the Blue Vipers who have struggled to score a few points." She observed Fish-face walking back to the stables. She wondered what his real name was. She did not have a chance to talk to the stable boy.

Prince Drago went to the side of the field and dug his fingers into the ground. He traced two horizontal lines right on his cheeks. "I *must* win!" His smoky blue eyes turned darker. His black hair was damp with sweat. He knew that missing one block could take away the victory. He extended his sword, aiming at Lummy.

"Why don't we just announce you the winner?" Lummy said to Drago.

"Princess! What are you waiting for?" added Drago in a mocking tone.

Martina blew the whistle. She felt some butterflies crashing the walls of her stomach. Concern whirled in her mind. She had heard about some serious Bladeking accidents. One time, an elite player was stabbed in the eye with the point of a sword and partially lost the vision in that eye. After that incident, helmets became mandatory for all professional fights. Another time, she heard of a kid breaking his leg, and it happened under strict supervision at the Ultimate Fight Summer Camp. The princess could not escape feeling worried about her brother. Drago had to fight two warriors at the same time. She was biting her nails, anxious for the game to be over. And she was not even thinking about all the incidental cuts at real battles where metal blades were used. That would have made her feel really sick and dizzy.

The green team captain positioned himself ready to face the blow and ward it off. "Come on! Shoot your sword," challenged Lummy. His now flat hair rested over his wet headband. The sun was beating its rays down. It was a hot and humid afternoon.

Drago did not say a word. He just frowned and engaged in an active fight. Swing after swing, it did not take longer than a minute for Drago to slash the point of his sword across the golden disk of Loretto. The dohket shattered like a cracker. "Piece of cake, Stick!" the prince sneered.

"*Sensational* battle by the blue captain. Ten sweet points for his team!" Martina sighed with relief.

Only Lummy remained in the game. Only Drago stood for his team. It was the final duel for the triumph and hopefully the last whistle.

"You can do it, brother!" encouraged Martina. She closely watched the action, her heart pumping fast.

Drago gave Lummy a bitter look. "Hey, loser! See if you can stop me. My sword is on fire!" scowled the prince. He drove his sword upward and with a loud screech, he sent a powerful thrust.

One sword pounding against the other, the two boys moved in circles around the middle of the field. Drago kept his position when he noticed that the sun came directly into Lummy's eyes.

"I can still win," said Lummy as he stumbled but managed to keep his feet on the ground. Squinting, he twisted and swung his sword hard at Drago. He put all his weight into that strike.

Drago saw the blade coming. He defended himself by side sliding the attack. He gave Lummy a dark look. He had to secure the victory. "You will lose!" Prince Drago breathed in. He went for another thrust.

But Lummy countered. "The game is mine!"

"Never!" Drago stepped forward and then he leapt into the air. His weapon plunged rapidly at Lummy, a perfect hit that caught him right on his chest.

Lummy reeled and fell. His gold dohket got pulverized. "Oh man! I was dazzled by the sun." He stood and moved off the field, looking down to the ground and trying to recover his sight.

Drago laughed in his face. "I'm the best!" He was bursting with pride as Martina announced the final score.

"The game has come to an end. The Blue Vipers win by forty points to thirty." Martina jumped with happiness as though she were at the championship final of the Kiston Bladeking Cup.

Drago walked to the middle of the yard. "Nobody can defeat Prince Drago!" he screamed, throwing his bandana up into the air. He hopped and bending his knees, he slid along the grass.

"Good game!" said Rocco. He cleaned the dust out of his glasses.

All the boys ran toward the prince, piling up. They laughed and cheered the end of their friendly match. Then Drago offered some refreshments for the group.

"You're a tough competitor to defeat," said Lummy, patting Drago on the shoulder.

"I know!" Drago took a big sip of his juice.

Martina also wanted to join the group. "Can I have some lemonade?"

"Of course, sis! But we're having some boys' talk here."

"Okay!" Martina got her cup. "I was a great referee. You're

welcome!" She curtsied and turned to her usual bench.

"Man, don't be rude. Your sister is so cute," Lummy said. His gaze drifted to the princess.

"You think?" Drago giggled. "It was so nice when the palace was just for me," added Drago, staring icily at Martina. The princess kept enjoying her drink away from the boys.

"Don't tell me, you're jealous of your sister?" teased Lummy.

"Are you crazy?" The two friends started walking around the field. Drago's glance flicked to his sister again. "Everybody protects little Martina as if she were a baby." The prince kicked a small rock with his black striped shoe.

"There must be a reason." Lummy kept eyeing Martina. Is the Eagle Sunday story true?" he whispered.

"Well … yes and no! She's not a witch, as of yet. But the weird bird part is true. I saw it!"

"Really?"

"With these same eyes," assured Drago, pulling down on one of his eyelids. "What bothers me is that my mother is so paranoid about Martina being normal that her nanny has to shadow her. Martina can only do homeschooling, and everything is for the princess! I'm sick of it." His face warmed.

"Relax, buddy! Do you want me to take her home with me?" Lummy winked.

"That wouldn't be a bad idea at all." Drago patted Lummy on his back. Shaking hands with his friends, the typical play day ended for the prince.

"Can I be a fighter next time?" insisted the princess as they walked inside the palace.

"Grrrrr! You really know how to be annoying." Drago stomped off down the blue corridor to his room.

Eager to use her new KIL200 at least once, Martina made her way up to her bedroom, hitting the stone balusters of the staircase. Her enormous suite was very luxurious. A stylish bed on a dais was at the center of the room. There was a door leading to her dressing room and another one to a sitting area. On the opposite side of the room, white carved doors opened up to a large balcony. There anyone could admire the main courtyard, a view that Drago complained he did not have.

Martina was tired that evening. All she needed was a quick bath to roll right into her cozy bed. The princess ducked under the covers. Soon she fell into a sweet sleep.

The night was quiet and cool. High ceilings and tall windows decorated the dark room.

Suddenly, a light cool breeze came through the balcony. A screech penetrated the moving drapery. The white fish eagle reappeared, swirling through the air. It flew straight into Martina's room, going for a landing on her bed footboard. The large bird rested its wings down. After a quiet moment, the big fowl turned into an old man. A few feathers remained on the white tunic of the stranger. He inched closer to the princess with the help of a silver staff. The long stick was topped with a dark fuchsia stone.

The old guy looked straight at Martina's closed eyes. Then, he slowly raised his staff, and pointing at the princess, he chanted with a raspy voice, *Forza Sabbina!*

Sparkling fuchsia light shot out from the staff, reaching Martina. Little crystals hovered over the princess. Some fell over the wooden box. The room became shiny and bright. But the girl was deeply dreaming.

The old man gently stroked Martina's black hair. "You were born with a natural gift: your eyes can project light. But now I have given you more ... the power to manipulate sand. With that power comes an important mission for Brightalia."

The magic gems spun around the bed, then up to the ceiling and lastly out to the balcony. In a flash, the white eagle shot itself into the dusky sky faster than a shooting star.

Only the weird man or fish eagle knew what happened to Martina that night!

CHAPTER THREE

"What was I dreaming about?" Martina asked the next morning. As much as she tried, she could not remember her dream. But she felt she had lived a great adventure that night. Then she noticed something strange on her bed.

Martina looked at the weird particles. Small, soft and thin grains were lying atop her white blanket. They had a light creamy color. She touched them and even tasted the tiny pieces. "It is sand!" shouted Martina. *How did it get on my bed? Who could it be? Is Drago playing another trick on me? Yes! It had to be my brother.* The princess was convinced. She put on her slippers and stared back at the sand. The soft grains had moved closer to her. *The wind! That's what it is.* Martina crossed to her balcony and shut the doors with one click. But again, the sand followed behind her, sliding along the floor.

Martina turned back and saw the snaky trail of thin grains. This time, she was certain it was not her brother or the wind. All color drained from her face. *Is this magical sand?* A knot rose in her throat. She could not swallow it. On more than one occasion, the princess had overheard the maidservants talking about magic and its danger. And the goodnight words that

Queen Constanza repeated every day immediately buzzed in her head: *Dear, if you see, feel or experience any sign of abnormal power, you must let me know right away. It is for your well-being and safety.*

Martina did not know what to do. What if her mom found out about the sand? Queen Constanza was petrified of magic. *She would have a fit! She will take it all away from me.* Martina walked from one end of her room to the other, clueless about what to do. What if her mother was right and magic could hurt her? One half of her was aghast, but the other one was curious.

On her tenth round, she spotted the simple timber box. Martina decided she wanted to discover more about the sand. She poured it into the wooden box. *This will be my magical secret*, she thought.

Night after night, Martina went to sleep hoping to get more sand under her pillows. She was anxious to understand her connection with the sand. Soon she realized that only when she dreamed about the beach, a small pile of sand appeared on her bed. It became a routine for Martina to wake up in the morning, grab the sand, and hide it.

The princess spent endless hours playing in her room with the sand. Mixing it with water, she created houses, columns, a mini statue and everything that she could stare at from her balcony. She became skillful at making sand figures with her hands. Yet she felt very lonely. She had no friends.

One day, some hope surfaced. Martina remembered about the stable boy. Maybe she could play with him, learn more about horses, or do anything fun. Have a friend! The princess rushed to the stables. She looked for Fish-face. But it was not her lucky Tuesday. The boy was only there on the weekends. Martina went back to her solitary room.

"Hello, my princess." Queen Constanza straightened her fine dress and entered Martina's bedroom. Her bodice was so tight she could barely breathe. The queen scanned the area for order and cleanliness.

Martina rushed to hug her mom. She threw a kick to a flowing skirt, shooting it directly into her dressing room. By good luck, it flew faster than her mom's eyes could see.

Queen Constanza gently put her arms around her daughter. "Your hair is so crinkly today." She turned to a dresser to look for a brush. But the queen accidentally pushed the wooden box to the floor.

Martina's heart pounded fast. She carefully picked up the box, gazing at it as she placed it back at the edge of the long dresser. *What should I do? Should I tell my mom about the sand now?* she mused. Her head was so confused. The princess simply continued combing her entangled hair. "It's just a little bit frizzy."

"I've scheduled the Etiquette and Protocol II class for you tomorrow," Queen Constanza smiled.

"Another one!" Martina rolled her eyes.

"Sweetie, the rules of good manners and proper etiquette are key to life in a royal society," explained Queen Constanza, stretching her neck as high as she could to show her best posture. "It's for your future."

Martina brushed her curls as rough as she could. "For my future? Ummm, for my future, I also want to ask you for something." Her voice let out a hint of craftiness.

"What could it be?"

"The beach! I want to go to the beach." It was not the first time the princess had asked her parents to take her.

The queen sat on the bed with her back perfectly straight. "Martina, you know that your father and I are preparing the Annual Harvest Fair, and we can't leave the palace right now."

The queen was trying to convince her husband not to cancel the Royal Pageant, the Tomato Contest, the Longest Bread Competition and all the additional village events that she had proposed for the occasion.

"But ... but ... Mother, please! Just for one day! We can go to that lonely sand island," Martina insisted, pulling hard on a lock of hair.

Queen Constanza observed her daughter's hairstyling technique. "I can't guarantee that it will be anytime soon, but I promise that I will fulfill your wish," assured Queen Constanza. She gave Martina a kiss on the forehead. In the doorway, she added, "Ah! I will request an Introduction to Beauty and Hair Design class for you. Trust me, you need it!"

"Sure, I can take some hair smoothing tips." Martina soon forgot all about the Royal Conversation Skills class, the Spell-Free Life tutorial, and the new Beauty and Poise courses she had to take. She lay on her bed daydreaming about her trip to the beach. Of course, she finished her clumsy hair job.

"Do you want to go to the garden?" Mercy said as she knocked on Martina's door. She was one of the maids at the palace. When Martina was born, Mercy had requested to become her babysitter. That was Mercy's expertise and what she mainly enjoyed doing. Martina always felt protected next to her nanny. Mercy was a competent and caring nursemaid. She was always looking after Martina. Nobody knew if it was because she cared or because of all the repeated times the queen had asked her to stalk the princess closely and even secretly.

The garden had flowers and trees from all over the world. At this time of the year, it was in full bloom sharing a pleasant aroma that spread across the entire palace. The picture-like garden sat on the back side of the hill and was impeccably maintained, as per the queen's compulsive wishes.

Martina felt like doing something different that afternoon. "The garden! Again! Almost every afternoon I play there," Martina moaned. "For years, I've been secluded in this palace."

"I know, Your Highness. It's for your protection."

"You're starting to sound like my mother." Martina pulled Mercy by the hand. "I've got it! I want you to show me the secret passages of the palace."

"Secret passages? There are none here!" chuckled Mercy, forcing her steps out of the room. Far from being good at it, Mercy made her best attempt to be creative for the princess. "I know … I can show you a secret view of Brightalia."

"A secret view?" repeated Martina, recovering her typical smile.

Mercy stopped, and lowering her voice, said, "The secret view is in the west of the palace." The nanny took a quick peek out into the hallway.

All the main bedrooms were on the west wing of the palace. At the end of the main blue corridor, there was the winding staircase that led to the crystal tower. Mercy mounted the stairway as though she were racing to get to a prize at the top. Martina had to skip steps to catch up with her. They headed out to the balcony. Martina stood on tiptoe to look at the horizon.

"Do you see the large extension of pastures to the far end of the land?" pointed out Mercy.

"Right past the stream?" said the princess, reaching as high as she could.

"Yes, Your Highness! Here is the only place in the palace where you can see Lusha Land." Mercy went on admiring the green view.

"Lusha? What is Lusha Land?" asked Martina.

"It's a rich land, west of the valley. It separates Brightalia from Castella. Most of our food was grown there. Our farmers took pride in their hard work to make their fields productive, but things have changed," said Mercy with a soft voice. "Unfortunately, it is a disputed land nowadays. I'm sure you will hear more about Lusha Land. Right now, just enjoy our secret view."

"No! Tell me more, please!"

"Well, let me start from the beginning. The Kingdom of Brightalia is made up of two major regions: the Enna Valley and Amo Island." Mercy held up her fingers as she named the kingdom areas. "The Enna Valley, or simply "the valley" as we call it, is the heart of Brightalia. It was the first territory conquered by King Amo, our first ruler. All trade and commerce activity takes place in the valley. Over time, its surrounding mountains became crowded with houses, leaving no space for growing crops and raising animals. This is why we need the plains of Lusha Land. Food shortages are one of the top crises of Brightalia."

"We need more land for farming!" Martina looked to the west as the daylight faded. "Can we plant somewhere else?"

"Woooh! That's another story for another day. Let's move to Amo Island. The beautiful deserted sand island is to the far east of Enna Valley. King Amo loved the ocean. The island was named in his honor. It's the best place to enjoy the beach in our kingdom, but honestly, there is nothing else to do there, and—"

"I'm thirsty to go there," interrupted Martina with a longing look.

"Why?" asked Mercy with curiosity.

"Just to see the ocean. Nothing else, right?"

"Right," nodded Mercy, raising an eyebrow.

They walked all around the tower, but it was getting dark. The secret view slowly disappeared in front of them.

"I'm going to prepare pasta for supper," added Mercy as they went back down to the main passageway.

Martina wrapped her arms around Mercy's waist. "You're the best!"

Martina returned to her bedroom. As she opened the door, the princess noticed that everything was out of place: her shoes in a corner, her gowns on the floor, her books on the bed, even some make-up that she had borrowed from her mom had been taken out of a drawer. She knew exactly who made the mess. She looked around the room, and at the usual corner, there was her wooden box, untouched and safe. Who could imagine that a simple box would contain magical sand?

But Drago was still suspicious. He would not stop until he discovered the secret of his sister. He approached the untidy room again.

Martina heard the sound of quick footsteps. She looked at the door with wide eyes. She slid under her bed as fast as she could.

This time, Drago went straight to the timber box. Martina's dress was sticking out. *Drago will know I am here!* thought the worried princess.

Drago stepped on Martina's dress but did not spot it.

The clever princess softly pulled the dress under the bed and quietly observed her brother.

Drago took the box. With a broad smile on his face, he examined all its plain sides. He then shook the small chest, but it did not make any sound as if it were empty. Convinced he had uncovered the mysterious secret, Drago tried to open it. Drago used all of his force time after time, but the wooden box seemed completely sealed. To his surprise, he could not find any possible way to lift the top of the magical chest. Disappointed, Drago dropped the box and kicked it against the wall. "I know she's hiding something," roared Drago as he slammed the bedroom door on his way out.

Martina could not believe what she saw. She crawled out from under the bed and picked up her magical box. She noticed that it did not have a single scratch or dent. As light as a ball of cotton, Martina opened the wooden box using only one of her fingers. All her sand was there. *Who gave me this box?* Martina wondered. Martina's simple wooden chest carried powers too. The princess put her magical box back into place. Her secret was safe, but her head was spinning.

CHAPTER FOUR

"Your Majesty, you won't believe what I just saw." General Althar, Chief of Army, strode inside the Diamond Office. His navy coat looked dusty. "I apologize for my unadvised entry."

"What brings you in such a hurry?" King Alessio turned his eyes away from the Brightalian newspaper. Skimming through *The Stone Street Gazette* was the typical start of the king's morning routine partnered with a cup of coffee in his other hand.

"Castella has done it again." The general took a deep breath and continued, "Our cows are dying. Also some of our pigs and turkeys."

Castella was a small kingdom surrounded by water. For centuries, it was a place that always lived in peace until one day, a tragedy happened. The king was murdered by his own brother, a greedy and war-hungry individual. Soon Castella became poor and in need of more land for housing. Its only option was Lusha Land. Not hard to guess that since then, the two kingdoms had been in constant battles for the coveted land. Brightalia wanted to plant and Castella had to build.

Neither kingdom could come to a fair agreement. Meeting after meeting, they had never been able to find a peaceful solution to the problem.

"What do you mean?" The king slammed the *Gazette* closed and directed all his attention to the general.

"One of their troops poisoned our water." Althar collapsed onto a chair.

"Can you be more specific?" demanded King Alessio, extending his arm.

"The Castellian army added poison to the drinking water of our cattle. They are all getting sick and dying," explained the Chief of Army.

King Alessio stood, reflecting in serious thought. He walked away from his desk to the Brightalia map hanging on the wall opposite his mahogany desk. "How do you know it was them?"

Althar pulled back his long-skirted coat and reached inside a small pocket on his white waistcoat. "I have the proof," said the general without doubt. He dragged a folded paper from his pocket and showed it to the king.

King Alessio unrolled the wrinkled paper and placed it on a table. It was a label with the skull and crossbones symbol. The king took a big sip of his already cold coffee and read, "Poison Extract – Product of Castella – Danger." He used the mug as a paper holder. There was a puzzled look on his face. "Where did you find this label?"

"Your Majesty, I walked all the pastures myself to look for clues. I didn't want to share any information with you until I felt one hundred percent sure it was them." Althar kept moving on his explanation.

"Stop rambling and tell me where the label came from." The king started to lose his usual patience.

"It was on an empty bottle next to one of the main water

fountains. I bent down to inspect the bottle, and when I looked across, I saw a Castellian soldier running away."

"He was coming back to pick up the bottle." The king rubbed his chin. "But he saw you."

"Just as it happened!" General Althar looked around avoiding eye contact with the king. "They did it at night. I have already established a soldier barrier along our fields."

"False traitors! They had agreed to stop the attacks on our fields as long as we do not touch any of the available lands," said King Alessio, his voice sounding deeper. "I will not allow them to ruin our food production." The king paused for a short moment and then faced the general directly. "Isn't our army securing our territory? Look at me, Althar." The king pointed a finger at the general.

"My apologies, Your Majesty." Althar turned to King Alessio. His face had gone pale. "They had temporarily backed off our borders for training," he added in an extremely low voice, only detectable by a mosquito passing by.

"Don't allow another Castellian to place a foot in our farms," ordered King Alessio with a frown of distrust. "Winter is soon approaching, and we can't afford to lose our crops too."

Castella's constant attacks on Brightalia were only a dirty strategy to force King Alessio to sign an agreement granting them most of Lusha Land.

"As you command." The russet-haired officer gave a respectful military salute and hurried out of the Diamond Office.

The king sighed as he went back to his desk. He did not notice that Martina had crept into the room through the back door and was sitting on the floor behind his opulent chair.

"Father, I want to learn more about Lusha Land," said the princess, swiveling her dad's chair around.

The king's heart jumped. "Sweetie, you're going to kill me one of these days." King Alessio helped Martina to her feet. "I don't think it's a good time right now to talk about Lusha."

"Please!" begged Martina with a pleading look. "Just tell me, what's the Frosty Treaty?" The princess plopped down onto the nearest chair as though she were a senior councilor.

"First of all, it's the Frost Treaty, and second, where did you hear about it?" asked the king, curious for the answer.

"I overheard a conversation at the Council hall yesterday. Some councilors seemed extremely concerned about the agreement." Martina managed to provide a coherent answer.

The king hesitated to explain the Lusha Land conflict to his daughter. "It's complicated, dear."

"I think I'm old enough to start learning about the issues that concern our kingdom." She was deeply serious.

"Well, you want to know. I'll tell you." The king rolled his chair closer to his daughter's. "The Frost Treaty says that available Lusha territory is frozen for use until there is an agreement on a frontier line."

There was a quizzical expression on Martina's face.

King Alessio smiled and translated. "Neither Brightalia nor Castella can touch any of the free lands in Lusha until we solve the border problem."

"And we need more space for farming."

"Exactly! Our poor families are already starving. With our cattle dying now, the situation only worsens."

"Why don't we just invade Lusha Land and forget about Castella?" suggested Drago as he swung the front doors open. He threw himself on a couch with his arms behind his head.

"Family debate!" The king turned his chair toward the leather sofa. "Son, I wish it could be that easy, but we can't break agreements. It would only bring worse consequences to our kingdom," explained the king. "In fact, Castella is the perfect example of what can happen to a kingdom that is incorrectly governed."

"What went wrong?" Martina was paying more attention than a councilor on the first day on the job.

"Castella was a nice kingdom, very rich. Now they only have a huge army. The king does not care about the needs of his citizens. They do not have schools, hospitals, and many homes have also been destroyed in wanton fights."

"That's why they need Lusha Land," guessed Martina, biting the inside of her cheek.

King Alessio nodded his head. "Exactly!" He looked concerned.

"Forget about the problems of Castella. Let's start planting in Lusha!" Drago moved next to a table and started sliding some pawns from a chessboard. He created a line of defense.

"Drago, that's not possible!" Martina made faces at her brother in disapproval. She did not understand Drago's attitude sometimes, or most of the time to be more realistic.

"Well! Let me propose something else." King Alessio stood to pick up a brochure from a bookshelf.

"As usual! You always ignore my comments," said Drago, tracing his fingers along the table.

"We're distributing vegetable baskets to our poor families," continued King Alessio. Opposite to the King of Castella, Alessio had always strived to be responsive to the needs of his people, even during rough times. Throughout the years, his dedication to the kingdom had helped him gain the respect and love of his people.

"I want to help!" Martina stared at the pamphlet for the date and location.

"Martina, I'd love for you to go, but you know that you can't leave the palace." King Alessio turned to Drago. "But your brother can help."

Drago kept moving the ivory chess statuettes. "Poof! Don't count on me."

"Why not?" asked the king, looking quite displeased.

Drago scowled and knocked down a rook. Then he removed the two queens from the board, and after that, he finally looked up and grumbled, "Why give free stuff to our people? Villagers must pay for their food. Aren't you the king? They are the ones who have to bring gifts to you!" Drago slid a chess piece to the center of the board.

"Ruling my kingdom is not a topic that I'm planning to discuss with you," said the king in a bossy voice. He moved the nicely carved king back to its start position.

"Fine. I'll help next year." Drago trod heavily, crossing through the tall oaken doors that led to the main corridor. "On February forty-first!" murmured the prince with a wry smile.

Martina rushed behind Drago. "I heard that."

Drago shrugged, "I don't care." He gave Martina a nasty look.

"I love you too, brother." Martina blew him a kiss. Just then, a heart made of sand landed on her hand. Trembling, she let the sand fall to the floor.

CHAPTER FIVE

A couple of months slipped by, and Martina continued to think about her long desired trip to the beach. By then, her secret ability had become her passion. She barely did anything else in the palace, but to play in her room. But there was one thing that still puzzled her. How did the heart of sand get into her hand? She wanted to discover how.

That night, the royal family was having supper in the turquoise dining salon. When the king was home, it was a family tradition to have an evening meal together and then spend some time in the music room. On this occasion, the dinner was an anticipated celebration of Martina's eighth birthday. It was an exquisite meal!

Queen Constanza entered the salon. "Is everything in place?" she asked, looking around the room.

Master Dante, the head butler, supervised the servants as they finished setting up the table. "We have taken care of all the details: the white dahlias, the silver plates, blue napkins…" He pointed at each of the items. "But we'll make any changes that you think necessary," added Master Dante politely.

"Everything looks lovely," replied the queen, touching the

engraving on a plate.

"Thank you, Your Majesty," said Master Dante, bowing to the queen.

"Tell me about the food."

"Cook Donato made all the preparations, and the kitchen maids are finishing the arrangements of the food trays."

"Very well done," Queen Constanza complimented. Suddenly, a repeated flash popped into her mind. "I hope we don't receive any unpleasant animal visits this year! Just to think about it, I get goose bumps." The queen could not help remembering the Presentation Day every time the birthday of her daughter approached.

Dante gulped hard. A knot strangled his throat. "M-m-me neither, Your Majesty," he stammered.

"Are all the background checks up to date?" asked the queen in a low voice.

Every servant had to submit a magic background check in order to work at the palace. Any person with the slightest history of magic would not be allowed to enter any of the premises of the royal family; no exceptions. All clearance letters had to be signed and stamped by a certified magic inspector.

"As you requested, all servants' files were validated this week," said Dante. His hands were shaky.

"Good job, Dante! Always keep an eye on those papers."

The butler bowed and ran up to Mercy, who was in line ready to enter the salon with the first wave of service, the vegetable soup. "Queen Constanza asked me about the servants' documents," he murmured as he nervously observed the king and children arriving in the dining room.

"Don't fret, Dante! I have everything under control," replied the nanny with a mumble. The procession started, and Mercy delivered the hot bowl to the princess.

After the soup, the appetizer service came, followed by the meat trays. With each wave of food, a procession of kitchen maids came into the room to serve the dishes.

King Alessio sat at the head of the table. He picked the largest piece of turkey. He was not too thin. But who would tell him that he was getting ... portly! "Martina, your birthday is coming up soon!" said the king eating his huge turkey leg. He could not enjoy a ribeye anymore. All the cows were gone thanks to Castella.

"Yes, we shall start planning the celebration," commented Queen Constanza ready to focus on a new extravagant dance. It was not a secret that she went overboard when planning an event. She tasted her carrots. "Delicious! It shall be a fantastic party this—"

"Another ball? I don't want a celebration or any presents," interrupted Martina in midsentence. She poked her fork into a piece of pork that never got to her mouth.

"What's wrong, my darling?" asked King Alessio with a surprised look. "You've barely touched your food and you don't want a present? I can manage the first one, but a kid who does not want a gift ... That's totally unheard of!"

"Do you feel fine?" Queen Constanza added. She eyed Mercy as she delivered a delightful bowl of fresh fruit to the table along with some sweet cakes.

"Yes! No! I mean, I'm okay, but what I really want for my birthday is to spend a day at the beach," sighed Martina. She grabbed a strawberry with her hand and threw it in her mouth and then a piece of apple followed by a couple of grapes.

King Alessio looked at Queen Constanza who soon remembered her conversation with Martina and the promise she had made to her daughter.

"We shall start packing!" Queen Constanza smiled. "But

please, next time use proper manners to eat your fruit!"

Martina's heart pounded with emotion. She held out her fist and jerked it down. *"Yeah!"* As the princess leaned in her chair, it flipped backward. She was down on the floor, and the only thing visible at the side of the table was the tip of her shoes.

"What a boring idea! The beach ... I'm not going anywhere," Drago blurted with a surly expression. "I must ask for something too. Maybe a horse!"

But nobody was paying attention to him. Instead, they were all laughing as Martina got up from the floor.

The fun moment continued at the music room while the family had tea, coffee, and some tasty desserts. Prince Drago played the piano in the meantime. He picked an array of traditional songs.

"I need to meet with Lord Campo early in the morning and then I'm free to go," said the king while having a cup of coffee on his blue armchair. The Emissary to Land Resources was working on the forty-fourth version of the agreement to try to settle the Lusha Land dispute.

"Have we signed the document?" asked Martina.

"Not yet!" said King Alessio, his voice grim. "But we keep pushing for that. Castella is watching closely, waiting for any opportunity to advance on our territory. They are hungry for our rich farmlands."

"I hope you can resolve the problem soon."

"Me too, sweetie," said the king, turning his gaze to his wife. "Right, honey?"

But Queen Constanza was not even listening. She was submerged in a paper, making an endless list of the bundle of things for the beach.

After the second song was over, King Alessio stood, and kissed his wife on the forehead. "I still need to sign a pile of approved job petitions before bed." He left the room with a loud yawn, but not before getting his hands on a chocolate cake – the secret recipe that was well kept at Troll Bakery.

The next morning, Martina was in her room. She was almost inside a wardrobe searching for her lilac hat.

"Good morning, princess! Here is your breakfast," announced Mercy as she entered the room.

"I can't find my beach hat!" screamed Martina, throwing things out of the armoire. She was not the most organized and tidy princess. Just then, a hat made of sand appeared on one of the wardrobe shelves. Hesitant, the princess extended her hand to touch it. It was plain sand, and the figure dissolved right away. Martina turned to Mercy. The violet color in her eyes had intensified. *Sand appears in my bed when I dream about the beach, but why are sand figures popping out of nowhere when I am awake? What is the weird sensation I am feeling in my eyes?*

"Are you okay?" asked Mercy. Her right eyebrow shot up. "Come out, and I'll help you." She set the tray on Martina's tea table and waited for the princess to move away from the armoire. "Have your egg and bread, and I will look for the hat," insisted the nanny.

At last, Martina sat at the table. But she kept looking at the wardrobe. She was afraid to tell Mercy about her secret. She did not know what Mercy thought about magic. Many questions went around and around in her head. *Can I control sand with my mind? Today can be a good test day!*

A light gust of wind crossed the room, and some of the sand got on the floor. "You haven't got to the beach, and there is already sand here! I need to clean this up." Mercy searched for the lilac hat, from the top to the bottom of the cabinet. "Found it!" she said, showing the hat to Martina.

The princess smiled and finished drinking her milk. "Good job!" she gave Mercy a thumbs-up.

"Let's go to your dressing room. A white beach dress is waiting for the princess," Mercy said fondly. "Have fun! Run, play, and get all wet."

"Yes! Fun!" Martina hurried into her dress. "I don't want to be too royal today. I want to be free!" After eight long years, Martina would enjoy her special day outside the palace.

They both sniggered.

Martina opened a drawer and gave a knitted rose to the nanny. "This is for you."

Mercy took the white flower and added it to one side of her hair. She was wearing a navy uniform. Her hair was pulled back into a perfectly made bun, and her shoes shone as if they were brand new. She gave a hug to the princess before leaving the room. At the doorway, she reminded her, "Have a lot of fun!"

"Yes!" Martina winked at her nanny.

Ready to leave, Martina anxiously peered out her balcony. The king's carriage was at the front doors. The servants carefully loaded all the beach belongings included in the queen's long list. Martina could not wait for the second that someone would call her name to go down to the JOR, which was how the servants called the king's coach in their frustrated longing for Just One Ride, one day. Of course, servants were not allowed to ride the luxury carriage.

And it was Queen Constanza who finally approached Martina saying, "Ready to go?"

"Yeah!" answered the girl who immediately dashed down-stairs and out the main door. Martina was pretty much bound to the tall rocky ramparts of the palace. She could only leave to be part of a kingdom event, and that was with at least two squires stepping on her shadow.

Right in front of her was the luxury carriage waiting for the family. The carriage was unique in style and the only one in the Brightalia Kingdom. Its top was made of glass. It was very spacious, allowing six people to comfortably share the passenger side. Bruno, the coachman, held the door open.

Soon the royal family was ready to depart!

Martina looked through the back window and waved goodbye to the servants who were kindly giving a farewell to the family too. She glanced at the palace as they went down the hill quickly approaching the village.

Prince Drago stood at the palace's front doors. He watched the royal carriage driving out of sight. "See ya!" he muttered. He walked inside, and his mind danced with selfish thoughts. "Perfect vacation day! A quiet palace full of servants just for me!"

CHAPTER SIX

The beach was not too far, and the ride was accompanied by a view that only Martina was enjoying. On one side of the street, the green mountains led the way, and on the opposite side, the surging waves freely hit the marble rocks of the sea stacks. The splashing effect sometimes reached the royal JOR, covering it with little drops. Each splash Martina captured as an imaginary shape. The sunlight added a rainbow illusion to her creation. She carefully observed the water while sitting still and waiting for what seemed to be an endless ride.

King Alessio continued adding ink to more petitions, while Queen Constanza devoured a creepy book, *The Underworld of Magic Phobia*.

The chain of mountains suddenly disappeared, and a long bridge appeared ahead of the carriage. The bridge was surrounded by open seawater. On the other end of the bridge was Amo Island, a lonely place famous for its sunsets. The fascinating island awaited the royal family to delight them with its crystal water. A special tent was already in place. It could be the least expected from the queen.

Martina quickly got out of the coach. Her first reaction was to open out her arms and close her eyes. She felt as though she had just been set free after a long sentence. There was no nanny or royal guard beside her, just a huge expanse of sand that she could not see the end of.

Not a footprint seemed to have touched the sand recently. Yet there was one sign of human life, an old person in a green canoe. Martina squinted. The bald man was not put off by the royal family's presence. He sat still with a fishing rod in the water. Martina took a mental picture of the old guy, who was soon out of sight.

At the tent, there were chairs, a long wood table, baskets with drinks and food, and even a special towel with Martina's initials. A violet umbrella with the kingdom's coat of arms was also in place for the princess. Martina grabbed her hat and sat on the sand far away from her umbrella. The sand had a light creamy color, almost white. She looked at it and gently touched it. That sand was similar to the one in her wooden box.

Yeah! This has gotta be my magical sand. Martina grabbed some wet sand and immediately built a rectangle with circular holes on all the sides. "A house!" she said to herself. The princess was ready to test her powers. She closed her eyes and imagined another rectangular figure. To her surprise, the unique house she had just fantasized stood next to the other one. It was perfectly made of sand. *Woohoo!*

Martina understood that she could manipulate sand with her mind. She tried one more time. And a few more times. She was fast, and the figures appeared identically in line one after the other. Then she stood and stared at her tiny village. *Only if they could be bigger and permanent!* That thought made her feel as if her eyes were going to project light. They gleamed an intense violet color.

King Alessio and Queen Constanza looked from a distance

at their daughter. They were very surprised to see how Martina was so skillful at making sand figures. Sure, they were oblivious to her powers.

King Alessio observed the vast amount of sand that surrounded the place. "I wish I could have some farms here! All this huge space wasted with sand," said the king, sitting at the table. A long sigh escaped his mouth.

Queen Constanza raised her eyes from the book, and scoffed, "You've got to be kidding me. Nothing will grow in here."

"I know, I know, darling. It's a crazy idea." The king snatched an apple from one of the panniers and gave it a big bite. "I feel I'm just running out of time, and I need to find a solution to ease the food shortage crisis."

"Martina, come join us for lunch," called Queen Constanza, reading her husband's mind. "Your father is hungry." The queen started pulling out food from a large bamboo basket.

"Juice for the princess," said King Alessio while serving his daughter a refreshing grape juice.

"Sure, Father!" Martina joined the table. She cleaned the sand off her hands. "Salted fish bites, yummy!" said the princess, savoring her food.

"And I brought something that you love too." Queen Constanza smiled back as she grabbed a container with fresh strawberries.

The family enjoyed their time together as well as the peace and calm felt at the beach. The sound of the waves was the melody to their meal.

"Martina," Queen Constanza wrinkled her forehead. "Where did you learn to make those sand figures?"

Martina did not know what to answer. She was afraid to tell about her secret powers. *Is it the right time now? My mom is going to flip from her chair!*

Queen Constanza kept looking at her daughter. She tapped her long nails on the table.

Martina breathed hard and quickly responded, "I have sand in my bedroom."

"Sand? Where did you get it from?" asked the king with a curious gaze.

"From my dreams! I create sand when I dream about the beach," explained Martina. "That's why I wanted to come here."

Queen Constanza's face turned to the color of milk. She tried to speak, but she could not get a word out of her mouth. Her throat had tightened with fear.

"And what else can you do?" the king asked, lowering his voice. He seemed very calm.

"I can build different figures with my sand," said the princess. She glanced at her mom. Was that a lie? She realized she had told the truth, but maybe not the whole truth.

Queen Constanza released a deep breath. Her teeth began to chatter.

"You have mastered the skills very well." King Alessio held Martina's hands. "Just remember … always use your talents to do good, to help others, to serve your kingdom," advised her dad with a mild look.

"I promise!" Martina raised her right hand. "I love my sand!" She grabbed her plate and briskly left for her umbrella before the queen could babble a word.

"Magical power? This cannot be happening to me!" The queen's voice faltered. "All I ever wanted was to have a normal life … a perfect family."

"Honey, we do have a normal life." King Alessio wiped the sweat off his forehead. "Martina is an ordinary kid with powers. Let's call them special talents."

Martina finished her delicious fruit and rested for a while.

She was enchanted by the relaxing view, and relieved to have shared her secret, partially!

"What is everybody going to say about our daughter? People will say she is a wit—"

"Stop it right there!" The king slammed his fists on the table. "You're the one who has to be a little bit more ... imperfect. Trust me, that's healthy!" He got a hold of a glass that was about to fall because of the wind.

"Why don't you read this book?" howled Queen Constanza. "I'm sure you will change your mind. Everything I do is to protect my children."

King Alessio could smell the book cover. It was an inch away from his nose. "Those books are driving you insane. Fling them away to the ocean! Do it. Do it now!" challenged the king with a loud shout. His quickening pulse could easily compete with any parade drums. He clearly heard the pounding of his heartbeats in his ears.

Queen Constanza hid the book behind her back. "I just want the best for my kids. I don't want anything bad to happen to them," said the queen with a broken voice. A flow of tears came to her eyes. "I can only see magic as something bad."

King Alessio saw Martina walking to the shore. She let the waves touch her feet. Then he faced his wife again. "I'm so sorry! Everything will be fine, sweetheart. Let Martina be a regular kid and discover her own powers," said King Alessio looking more relaxed and grabbing the queen's hand under the table. "Magic can be good. It depends on how you use it."

"Her powers are starting to show! I did not expect it to be this soon. I always denied that she had ... special talents," Queen Constanza sighed. She could not hide her concerned look. "Should we keep the secret?"

The king shook his head. "Martina will know when it is the

right time to reveal her magic," King Alessio calmly assured her.

The waves kept pushing Martina away from the seashore. She tried to swim but did not make headway. She could scarcely see her umbrella. The ocean felt cooler than before, and the heavy water darkened around the princess. She yelped a tearful, "Daddy!" But her shrill scream got lost in the agitated waves, never reaching the surface. Her words had transformed into mute bubbles.

"What about Drago?" asked Queen Constanza. Her heart was beating fast. "Does he have powers too?"

"Honestly, I don't think so. There have been no tangible manifestations. Well, as of now." The king went on, "We just need to watch him closer."

"And school? Oh my goodness! I'm going to die if I have to take Martina to EWA!" A torrent of questions crashed the queen's head.

"You bring up a good point! I'll look into Elithard Wizardry Academy," suggested King Alessio, ignoring his wife's magic phobia.

Elithard Wizardry Academy, or EWA, was the best wizardry school. It was only four hours away from Brightalia. It had recently got its license from the Segna Association of Master Wizards. It also offered a new summer exchange program to the Blue Cryptic Mount, home of the enigmatic association. Only kids with special powers were admitted to the academy.

Queen Constanza was not too convinced about the idea. It only brought chills to her bones.

"At EWA, Martina can have the right guidance to learn how

to use and control her powers. It will be a great experience for her." The king's excited voice sounded like a teenager talking about his new retractable KIL700 sword.

"Honey, I need time. It's too much to digest in a single day."

"All the courses that Martina has taken at home prevent her from learning magic," added the king with a grunt. "Not to insult your good intentions."

"Those are excellent classes." Queen Constanza turned her gaze away from her husband.

Meanwhile, Martina struggled to keep her mouth at water level. She could not focus anymore. Her eyes looked empty. Her arms grew weary from her endless windmilling. The thrashing waves sank the princess downward and deeper one and many times. The salty water soon traveled a long way in her system. Her lungs started to ache. At last, tiredness took over her entire body. After what seemed an eternal battle, Martina's eyes closed, surrendering to the brave ocean. She touched the seabed.

King Alessio paused in thought. "Constanza, I understand your fear, and I want everybody to be happy and at peace. Let me find out about EWA, just to be informed," he proposed. "In the meantime, I want you to do the extra effort and add real magic courses as part of Martina's homeschooling program. Agreed?"

Another long sigh escaped Queen Constanza's red lips. Her glamour made it to the beach too. "Agreed," the beautiful queen finally said.

Unexpectedly, a high wind blew the fruit basket and with it, the rest of the items from the wood table. Everything crashed into a nearby rock in a heap. The highly stretched wings of a bird flapped various times as it swooped down to the ocean. Faster than a boulder tossed from a siege engine, the fowl took a straight dive into the water.

King Alessio jerked his head at the beach. "Martina!" His shout resonated across the island. He jumped and sprang up from his chair. In a split second, he got to the shore.

"My daughter! I don't see her!" howled the queen. She made a quick attempt to get up, but her legs were numb with nervousness.

The white fish eagle yanked the princess upward into the air. Its claws tied around Martina's shoulders. Her body hung sprawling. The fowl cawed and made a soft landing next to the king. His eyes popped as the bird left Martina lifeless on the warm sand. The eagle gently tapped its beak on the princess's chest. Its dazzling fuchsia eyes met the king's grave gaze. With another wail, the white bird snapped its wings and glided away, crossing the ocean waters.

Queen Constanza clomped to the beach. Her legs were shaky. "Is she breathing?" asked the queen, bursting into tears. Her heart skipped a dozen beats when she saw her daughter's purple lips.

Martina shivered. Uncontrollable cold chills traveled along her spine. Her wet skin was plastered with sand. King Alessio rapidly started giving a couple of breaths to the princess. Then, he applied pressure on her chest several times. "Breathe, sweetie, breathe!" desperately begged the king.

With every push in the center of Martina's chest, the queen cried the correct count of the beats. "Stayin' alive. Stayin' alive!"

After a few agonizing minutes, Martina spewed out a mouthful of salt water, taking her first breath of fresh air. She opened her dazed eyes. "Father!" the princess managed to say, gasping for more air. She gave a blank stare at the king.

King Alessio's heart sank back in place. He gulped hard, his throat dry. "I thought I had lost you!"

Queen Constanza fell down in happy tears. "I love you more than my own life." She rested her head on Martina's legs.

The gleaming sun started to set. It slowly disappeared in the water as the shiny stars peeked out under the night sky. King Alessio and Queen Constanza let Martina rest for a little bit longer while they got ready to leave the beach. But the eagle appeared next to the princess. The white bird transformed into the old man. He smiled at the young girl.

Martina stared at him with amazement. "Who are you? You were at the sea this morning," Martina said in a faint voice.

The bald guy smiled one more time. He leaned on his long staff and moved a few steps closer to the princess, giving her a prophecy. "One day you will save your kingdom, but only if you save a special boy first." He then disappeared as silently as he appeared. The fish eagle soared up into the air, flew past the beach bridge, and vanished among the clouds.

"Wait! Wait!" cried Martina. She tried to lift an arm, but it seemed heavier than an anvil. She was too weak. How was she going to save someone if she could not even save herself? And a special boy ... What did the old man mean? She had no idea where to start looking.

The royal couple was ready to start the journey back home. King Alessio carried Martina in his arms. She felt the strong steps of her dad plunging into the sand. The princess hoped that one day she could come back and build more.

As the royal carriage drove away, Martina took a last glance at the beach. She saw how most of the houses had already vanished with the sea breeze. But she was tired and quickly fell asleep. She dreamed vividly as fresh oxygen pumped into her brain. Her sick stomach started to recover during the silent ride. It was noiseless inside the JOR. The king and queen did not utter a single sound until they drove up the hill and into Diamond Palace.

"Not a comment on what happened," the king muttered. It took a while for the king to drain the tense moments out of his mind.

Queen Constanza simply nodded in agreement.

At the queen's reception room, a birthday cake waited for the princess. A big number eight sat on top of the cake. When the family entered the room, a choir started singing "Happy Birthday". They were all the palace servants. Drago accompanied the song by playing the piano.

"Congratulations, little sister," Drago said as he concluded his cheerful melody.

"Happy birthday, my sweet daughter!" Queen Constanza gave a kiss to the princess. "I could not have lived this day without you."

"May all your wishes and dreams come true," added King Alessio. "With good health and far away from danger," he coughed.

Martina opened her arms around her parents and crushed them in a hug. "I'll never forget this day!"

Prince Drago wrapped around his family. He let a big smile fill his face.

"What a day!" said Martina without letting go of her parents.

After being at the bottom of the ocean, rescued by a fish eagle, and revived by her dad, Martina had learned that her magical powers were stronger than she thought. She could use her imagination to control sand. And she was told more. A prophecy!

What could the princess create using her secret abilities? And where could she find the special boy? She only hoped it would not be troublesome to continue uncovering her magic.

CHAPTER SEVEN

Five years passed, and the princess became an attractive teenager. Her long eyelashes embellished her deep violet eyes. Each day, they shone even more. Her wavy hair had grown long curls. Her silky hair continued to have its vivid black color, of course, only to be admired by the servants of the palace. At age thirteen, the young lady barely knew her town. Queen Constanza had allowed her daughter to take a few "talent" classes at home, but she had not overcome her fear about sending Martina to EWA. The princess kept talking about a special boy. It was hard to find him if she could only search in the palace! As far as friends, there were not too many options among the servants. Enzo never returned to the stables. He got a job at a farm closer to his home.

For Drago, it had been a wild ride of adventures. The tall young man had scrutinized every hole on the streets of Enna Valley. With his soft black hair and gloomy blue eyes, one could say that he was somewhat good looking, but he continued to lack the charming personality of his sister. He was very athletic, passionate about music and sports, but he was also risky and aggressive at times. His selfishness overcame him.

On the positive side, he had stopped trying to discover what Martina hid in her mysterious secret box. But there was always a distance between the siblings. Sometimes they even acted as complete strangers, ignoring the presence of each other. For a long time, Martina tried to get closer to him, but Drago always rejected her. Eventually, she got accustomed to the growing distance between them. However, she never stopped loving and caring about her only brother.

The food crisis had gone nowhere close to a solution. Every day, there were more people in the streets begging for food. The kingdom not only remained very active with its problems but with its events as well. Brightalia was hosting the Annual Horse Master Competition. It had been a long time since the kingdom had the honor to welcome other dynasties.

Queen Constanza, well known for her cordial and warm hospitality, did not disappoint her honorable guests. Her extravagance was also present. At the Brightalia Coliseum, the field was decorated with kingdom flags, the entrance was renovated, a designated area for the royal families was for the first time created, and a major horse stable was rebuilt. There were more than one hundred huge horse statues around the arena.

Prince Drago was excited about the competition. He was old enough to ride for the first time. It was his memorable moment to show his pride and conquer the victory at home. He had practiced intensely. He had trained in rivers, swamps, and up rocky mountains. Cross-country was his passion. For a competitive guy like him, there could be no more ambitious goal than to win the Horse Master trophy. For three days, Brightalia became the center of attention of all neighboring kingdoms.

The Horse Master inauguration ceremony was about to begin. King Alessio, Queen Constanza, and Martina watched the show at the royal platform. Just like a clapper in a bell, Martina agitatedly swung her hands at the crowd. She did not want to miss anybody. She was so happy to have left the palace.

"Martina, calm down," whispered the queen as she and King Alessio royally greeted their people.

Judges were at their designated locations. Slapping drums began playing. Each kingdom presented its riders and horses. The kingdoms' flags led the way to their riders. Castella was the second kingdom to enter the field. Taunts and jeers came from the benches. At last, it was the host kingdom. Prince Drago entered the field riding his favorite black horse, Dark Knight, and leading his new mare, White Diamond. His outfit was impeccable – a dark wool cloak, royal blue tunic with accents in brass, armor belt, pearl breeches, kingdom helmet, and black high boots. He received a thundering ovation from the crowd. He pranced along the ring like a famous gladiator. Drago greeted the audience making a 'V' with his fingers, way up high. His face could not hide his love for the popular applause.

King Alessio and Queen Constanza went down to the field to cut the royal ribbon. It marked the official start of the competitions. Fireworks illuminated the sky as the band performed its final show.

Everything was in place for the equestrian triathlon. Everybody hoped it would be a few days filled with energy and enthusiasm. The order of the competition phases was changed to accomplish this goal. After the alarming number of rider deaths the previous year, the challenging cross-country and the exciting show jumping were finally phased out. Cross-country became the first horse trail followed by the artistic Dressage event. The Show Jumping remained as the last trial. Another change was the inclusion of more than one horse per rider after looking at the safety of the animals too. But the measures were relative. The courses were not going to be any easier. Riders almost choked after they walked the cross-country wild terrain.

Martina watched Drago saddled up his black stallion, Dark Knight. She knew her brother loved cross-country, but she was still concerned about the risky field. Drago knew the land so well that she feared he would go faster than he should.

This was the race to prove the endurance, speed, and jumping ability of the horse while guiding the equine through natural obstacles like thick logs, tall stone walls, deep ditches, muddy bogs, narrow rivers, and even dark tunnels. This year, a hanging bridge was also included in the challenging trail.

Drago and Dark Knight trotted to the warm-up area. The four-year-old horse was relaxed and responsive. Drago knew it was going to be a rigorous test. They both needed to be bold and brave. Drago's mind was set to complete the course on time and with as few penalties as possible. He had already heard that two horses refused to cross the hanging bridge and that jump seven was a killer, a fence with a ditch in front. That was the easy part. It was located on the side of a steep hill.

It was about time. One more rider, and then it was the prince's turn. Drago glanced at the start box. Prince Filippo, from Castella, waited there for the countdown. The previous competitor, Duke Lew, was about to exit the field.

"Five, four, three, two, one! Have a good ride!" said the timekeeper.

Drago could see how Filippo's horse leapt over the first log fence and landed like a champ. They engaged in a rhythmical canter over the next few fences with ease. But that was about it.

Then they went deep into the forest. Drago noticed Filippo was confident and demonstrated control of his movements. The Prince of Brightalia continued with his warm-up routine.

After ten minutes and twelve seconds to be exact, Prince Filippo emerged from the forest crossing the finish line. He was all covered in mud. White-faced, but happy he proudly raised his hand and saluted the multitude. Some mild applause came from the benches. Filippo made it through what he considered his weakest event.

Martina sprinted to the front of the royal platform as Drago and his mount approached the start box. "This race is yours, brother!" cheered the princess in support.

Drago turned his head and winked at his sister. "Don't worry. I'm the best!" He frowned and focused back on the challenge ahead of him.

The competition was running a bit behind. Prince Drago hoped he could still finish with enough sunlight. He was the last rider. He mastered cross-country very well so he wanted an outstanding performance. All the other riders had fallen at some point and had been forced to walk their horses through the hard jumps. Drago knew that if he stayed at a canter the entire course, he would be ahead.

"Five, four, three, two, one! Enjoy the journey, Your Highness!" chanted the timekeeper. He could only catch a glimpse of the trail of dust behind the fast horse.

Dark Knight cantered out of the start box and popped over the double log fence with a perfect landing. "That's my buddy!" complimented Drago with a brief patting on the crest. They soared over the second fence – a combination of stonewalls. The nimble equine locked into a nice gallop after going down a bank. The leafy vegetation of the woodland began to be seen. It was getting breezy and cool. The wind made Drago pucker his forehead. Still, he bustled over more fences like a war hero on his trusty stallion. Right in front of them, the tunnel became visible. Coming out from pure darkness onto the top of a mound was quite a panic scene. There was some resistance and a loud bellow from Dark Knight. But Drago did not hesitate a second longer. They did not delay to cross it with a rapid gait.

"Great job, buddy. We'll make it!" declared the prince. In spite of his audacity, Drago knew he was close to the killer fence. Jump seven eliminated the unlucky riders from the East Kingdoms. Well, all but one. Duke Lew managed to remain in the competition. The judges admitted he was a skillful rider.

Drago knew he had to empty his mind and overcome any feeling of dread. And that was exactly what he did. They flew over the killer jump. Drago felt the stirrups pressing up into his boots as his body was suspended in the air. The nonsense idea of defying gravity did not seem too crazy at that point. He really made his best attempt while trying to get an eye on the landing. Dark Knight touched the ground eagerly with a forward canter. Drago felt relief. He steered toward the next set of flags with good control of the terrain. Dark Knight was settled. The stream was refreshing and caught the horse with a fantastic rhythm. They vaulted over the wet fence and bounced out of the creek with just a sideways slip. But Drago did not slow down. Dark Knight had to awkwardly recover his balance as they rode away from the swampy field. The next challenge was the intimidating hanging bridge. This time, Dark Knight approached the edge with clear hesitation. The horse's head shot up higher than a giraffe. Yet Drago was not ready to stop.

"Keep moving, my friend!" The prince spurred the equine to make it lunge forward. They loped their way over the tall waterfall. The creak of the wood was not the best companion sound. Dark Knight's ears swung in all directions just like a sword in a Bladeking game. Drago gave him a deserved break. They cantered to the next table fence. Back to a comfortable gait, they jumped the rest of the course with total control. The arena was ahead of them. The crowds were on their feet. Martina's heart rested when she saw the black stallion crossing the finish line. Drago removed his helmet and tossed it into the stands.

The multitude erupted with applause yelling, "Brightalia! Brightalia!"

Prince Drago left the field with a broad smile on his face. He did not exceed the optimum time. And to his satisfaction, he made it to the top with the best score of the competition.

Back at the palace, King Alessio and Queen Constanza celebrated and congratulated Drago.

"Your mom and I are very proud of you, son," said King Alessio.

"Thank you, Father!" Prince Drago twisted his mouth into a gleeful smile.

Queen Constanza walked toward Drago. "I'll not miss a single competition!" added the queen, hugging her son.

That night it was somewhat different. Drago showed a great sense of affection to his parents and sister. Martina received a couple of kisses from her brother, and a short dance that she would have never expected.

Prince Drago was shining. It was his night. "I'll bring home the trophy!" he assured.

CHAPTER EIGHT

Prince Drago arrived early at the barn. It was almost day-light. Only the stable boys were there.

"Good morning, Your Highness!" said Enzo as he forked some hay into the last stall. The poor villager was there too. His mom, Julia, continued her long battle with her lung condition. Every day, it was more difficult to find the Jentha herb. The tea made from its dried leaves was the best remedy to cure breathing problems. The weak infusions that she received every week were not enough, and the level of oxygen in her blood continued to go down. If Julia did not find more Jentha herb, she would soon have to change her head seamstress position at Casa Victtoria for bed at home. Enzo knew he had to chase any job opportunity ahead of him.

"Is that you?" asked Drago, raising his gaze. "Fish-face?" The prince offered him a silly smile.

"Enzo is here," he clarified, continuing with his task. "Early and happy just like your mare."

Drago walked over to check on White Diamond. The mare snorted, holding her head up. "Hello, Snowie. Today is your big day!" said Drago, looking at her mane. Drago trusted Martina.

He followed her suggestion to take White Diamond for the Dressage trial.

"Did you give her the yellow potion?" asked Drago.

"Five minutes ago," said Enzo, filling up a water tank. "Does the potion have sugar?" He carried the heavy tank and watched White Diamond. "She's jumpy! I can take some of that and finish my job faster than an octopus."

"That's exactly what I don't need." Drago crossed his arms and stared at how the excited mare ran around like a dog chasing its tail. "She'd better relax!" said Drago not in a happy tone. He vaulted into the saddle and rested his feet firm on the stirrups. After jigging sideways, they made it to the warm-up area. The white mare was totally overwhelmed by the busy environment. Drago had to regain control. The good part was that he still had time.

The band played next to the royal platform. At the entrance was a stone board displaying the results of the cross-country races. The second demonstration was scheduled to begin sharply at eight o'clock. Dressage was the artistic phase of the competition, testing how obedient and responsive a horse is to his rider. Completing classic movements and fancy footwork on the flat were the key elements in the exhibition. Not particularly the most attractive event for Drago. Even so, nobody could deny that he had trained hard to perform at this event. Tempting to say, many believed Filippo was the master at this discipline.

Letters were in place at their assigned positions in the enclosed arena. The king selected the letters D-R-A-G-O in honor of his son. It was a small routine, but still, all horses needed to memorize the pre-determined movements.

Prince Filippo offered an impressive demonstration as

anticipated. His horse was very attentive and supple. They moved in a straight line to the start of the routine. They mastered every transition, completing the pattern in the proper order. The highlight was a piaffe. The horse really seemed to remain on the spot while maintaining this elevated trot. The relaxed and effort-free appearance when performing the movements captivated the judges. The spectators showed some sympathy with a round of applause. Filippo jogged around the arena greeting his few followers.

Martina could not stay in her seat any longer. She rushed to the warm-up area looking for Drago. She sensed something but could not explain what it was. Dressage was the type of ride she enjoyed, but she knew Drago found it boring. He preferred the unexpected action of galloping through the open fields. "Are you ready? Only one competitor ahead of you."

White Diamond nickered at Martina. "Hello, girl!" By then she was fairly calm and confident.

"It's not what you see now. Your favorite mare was tense and scared. It's taken me quite some time to make her bend and move easily." Drago kept circling with impatience. "It's frustrating! Why did I listen to you?" roared the prince.

"Trust me! White Diamond is good at this." Martina tried to get Drago to relax. Although, the truth was that she was more anxious than her brother. Drago was attempting his best, but maybe his personality was not a good fit for this event.

"I must go now."

"Good luck! You'll do great," said Martina with hope and concern at the same time.

Prince Drago got to the main arena. The elegant mare by itself was a total exhibition. On her forehead, a bright diamond sparkled with the sunlight. Her enchantment got overthrown as soon as people started clapping. Her ears twitched up stiffer than a wall. Drago smiled as he struggled to make her move near the first letter.

Martina's eyebrows shot up. She was confident White Diamond was more than capable of getting a top score. Peculiarly, today did not seem like a good day.

"Come on, Snowie! Show your best moves." Drago would never give up on his ambitious goal of winning the trophy. Ultimately, he showed good control of his mare as she gracefully danced around the first letter. Nice movements for the second letter, but some resistance at the end. White Diamond ended the show with a fancy halt. It was safe to say that it was not the best test, but still good to get a decent score.

Not for Drago, he could not believe he was down to second place. He was furious at his performance. He felt all his effort was useless. He left the field without greeting the audience. People clapped showing support to the host kingdom, but many were surprised that the victory could be taken away from Prince Drago. He walked to the stables, threw his helmet against a wall, and went home. He acted as if he had been eliminated from the competition. He was used to being the winner, the champion, the first in everything.

Martina ran to the stalls, but Drago was gone. She spotted White Diamond still cooling off as Enzo poured some water for the overwhelmed mare. "Fish-Face?"

King Alessio and Queen Constanza immediately arrived looking for their son.

"Where's Drago?" Queen Constanza gave a 360-degree glance at the area.

"Gone with the brisk wind in one of the royal carriages!" described Enzo.

The king's carriage showed at the back exit. Bruno hurried out of his seat. "Your Majesty! I'm glad I found you here," said the coachman, his voice shaky.

"What's the matter, Bruno?" King Alessio had no clue as to the grim face.

Enzo raised his ears higher than the horses as he continued his cleaning duties.

"Farmers and villagers banded together at the main entrance to protest." Bruno lowered his voice and moved closer to the king. "They carry signs asking for food and think that all the money spent on this fancy event should have been invested in agriculture."

"It's not about money. It's all about land," clarified the king. Pressing thoughts ran through his mind. "This is getting out of hand. I need a solution faster than yesterday." Very unusual, he was the first one to enter the coach.

"The kingdom events do not interfere in any way with the farming crisis," added the queen, following behind her husband. She would never sacrifice her glamorous shows. They kept her alive.

Martina did not say a single word. But she smiled and waved goodbye to Enzo as she entered the carriage.

It was a silent ride home and night.

On a bright and sunny Sunday, what everybody was waiting for would shortly begin. The third and final event was taking the stage – the Show Jumping competition. Much speculation and rumors flowed among the people as to who the lucky winner was going to be after the disappointing second place of Prince Drago in the Dressage trial. Was the Horse Master trophy going to stay in Brightalia or travel to Castella? Everybody knew that the battle was going to be between Prince Drago and Prince Filippo. The rider with the lowest combined score at the end of the triathlon would take home the trophy and distinguished blue ribbon. Only three competitors made it to the nail-biting final race.

The obstacle course was meticulously prepared. A variety of fences differing in height, width, and technicality were selected to test the horses' balance and adjustability. The course designer did an excellent job at blending the level of difficulty into the arrangement of the floating jumps. Yes! Some jumps were suspended in the air, just above the ground. They gently moved from side to side or up and down. It was a tradition that almost caused Queen Constanza a heart attack, but she could not break it.

The culture of the kingdom was also incorporated into the decoration of each obstacle – carved columns, monster figures, arches, and miraculously a white eagle. It was an authentic work of art. It was then up to the riders and horses to complete the course without knocking down any of the fences and obtain the fastest time.

Drago was very anxious but confident. He really trusted Dark Knight and knew he had all the muscular strength, cardiovascular endurance, and training needed for an excellent performance. *I must be the champion!* Drago thought with certainty. He could not stand being defeated.

"It was a nice performance yesterday." Filippo passed by Drago, cleaning the dust off his cloak.

Drago pretended not to listen. He tightened the saddle in place.

"Castella is ready to celebrate my victory!" Filippo said in his taunting voice.

This time, Drago could not ignore Filippo. He furiously snarled, "Never! The Master trophy will be mine! Mine, and only mine!" Drago repeated as he walked away from Filippo.

His blood boiled like an erupting volcano.

Filippo laughed out loud. "With a magic leap of luck ... maybe!"

The Show Jumping started, and Drago looked from a distance still burning at Filippo's words. He was the last participant as usual. The scores were very tight. To add another layer of difficulty, riders were not allowed to walk the field before the competition.

Sitting on his horse, Duke Lew was ready to ride out. He was the first rider, followed by Filippo and then Drago. Lew knew that a single mistake could mean losing the championship. The course needed to be completed as quickly as possible without making any errors. It was definitely going to be a race for the best time. His horse looked calm. They started off with a great rhythm. They vaulted safely and with a good pace. Lew's jumps were very clean except for one. He tripped over one of the floating fences, but he did not knock down any of the poles. He managed a safe landing after the ditch. It was safe to say that Duke Lew put on a good routine.

Drago headed to the warm-up area and jumped some practice fences. The show jumping ring was running a bit behind schedule. He and Dark Knight were prepared to face a tough ride.

Martina was restlessly waiting. Filippo was the toughest competitor for Prince Drago to beat, and he had a good record at show jumping. The royal platform space suddenly got too small for her. She quickly ran to the stables looking for Enzo.

"Fish-face!" Martina called several times. She did not see Enzo. "This guy is like a ghost," said the princess, talking to herself.

Martina decided to scramble along the crowd. She noticed that some people moved away when they saw her coming, and some townswomen began to murmur. But she did not care and continued climbing benches. At last, she recognized some friendly faces. "Lummy … Rocco! I'm so glad I found you," said Martina with a smile as she made it to a top corner stand.

"Hey, Princess! Nice to see you," responded Lummy, making some space for Martina to sit.

"How is your brother?" asked Rocco. His glasses flashed with the sunlight. He and his friend had stopped going to visit Drago. They claimed Diamond Palace was too far from their houses, but the truth was that they got tired of always having to do what Drago wanted. Every play day, the story repeated.

"I hope well. He wasn't very pleased yesterday."

It was time! Prince Filippo was at the start line. He was confident that he could improve the time and obtain a higher score than Duke Lew. Filippo was determined to give his best performance. Uttering a long whinny, the horse cantered past the start line. They breezed over the first sea monster rail. The second jump was a long combination of three obstacles, but they managed to complete it without knocking down a single bar. They got into a nice gallop and soared over a brick wall with total control of the landing. Their ride was so smooth it seemed effortless. The last floating jump was executed with great boldness. They made it to the final line! It was, in fact, his best race. His score, a new record! Filippo was ready to take the Horse Master trophy home.

Martina covered her face with her hands. "Oh no!" She felt like crying. She did not want to listen to the deafening cheers.

"Chill! Drago will make it to the top," encouraged Lummy.

"He's an excellent rider."

Martina was nervous. She knew her brother very well. Drago would risk his life even if it were to win a single coin for a race in his backyard. "I just hope he stays under control."

Rocco sipped his juice. "It'll be tough," said the boy in a quiet whisper.

Prince Filippo went to the back of the arena, hooting and laughing at Drago. His victorious ego arose when he walked past his rival. "Impossible to beat this champion!" said the prince, bragging about his horse-riding expertise.

Drago ignored Filippo, who was playing him with the same level of arrogance. He focused on his upcoming final race. He knew that he had to push Dark Knight to his fullest potential. It seemed as if Dark Knight also knew that a great effort was required to win the competition. Drago was the only competitor left to take away first place from Filippo. It was going to be extremely hard to improve on Filippo's score. It was the endeavor to triumph.

With reins in his hands, the last competitor got to the start line in a natural trot. Martina and Drago's friends chanted his name over and over. "Drago of Brightalia! Drago of Brightalia!"

Little by little, the rest of the throng joined the acclamation. Enzo, who was sent to buy more hay, rushed closer to the arena. He could not miss the show. King Alessio stood and moved to the front edge of the platform. The queen just pressed her hands against her chest.

Drago took a determined breath. He dug his spurs into Dark Knight, and with a firm move of the reins, declared bravely, "Run Knight ... run Knight ..." A loud neigh was heard as Dark Knight dashed through the start line. Drago raced toward the first jump leaping over the sea monster rail as a legendary jockey. It was perfectly executed! At the second fence, Drago continued pushing Dark Knight to run faster and faster. This jump was the most difficult one, a floating joker. But they were very alert, and the tricky fence did not confuse them. With a long hop, they scuttled over the rustic rail. Drago obtained a clean performance. His mind was set to be the winner.

"Go Knight, go! Faster, faster, we can do this!" shouted Drago. They locked into a flashy gallop as they flew over the next set of jumps. The race seemed tight. The prince felt as though he were on a time bomb. Sweat crossed his entire forehead. They kept racking more floating fences with true boldness and extreme precision. After crossing the ditch of the white eagle jump, Drago gave his final command to Dark Knight to increase his speed even more. Ahead there was only one more obstacle. Drago was not thinking about danger. He just wanted to win. Dark Knight sprinted at full speed over the last floating jump, another perfect landing to cross the finish line in an agitated gallop. Did he break Filippo's new record?

The entire stadium screamed for victory. Martina nervously turned to the stone board.

"He did it?" asked Lummy.

"I don't know!" Martina bit her lip in worry. Drago's score was still missing.

"Stop, please!" screamed Rocco, pointing at the arena.

The race was officially over. Something was wrong. Drago pulled back on the horse's rein hard, but Dark Knight was out of control. He struggled to hold his black stallion together. He could not make him stop. They were getting too close to the first fence again.

"Please stop!" howled Martina with despair.

Drago's eyes popped out. He was incapable of getting Dark Knight to respond to his stop command. The wild beast was totally rebellious and insubordinate. Dark Knight ran rampant to the sea monster rail. Drago did not have a choice, but to hastily bounce over the obstacle. They were too low!

A collective groan came from the entire stadium.

The horse hit the poles and did not have enough time to fully recover from the jump. Dark Knight landed on his forelegs sliding along the arena. A big cloud of dust covered most of the field. Drago flew off the horse like a cannon ball and hit a fence. A painful crash! His helmet broke. He ended with a thud, face down on the ground.

Then he collapsed!

A hush invaded the entire arena. Everybody was in disbelief.

King Alessio quickly ran to the field. He bent over Drago and turned him over. "Son, respond please!" His face was as white as a sheet of paper.

Queen Constanza was in complete shock. Martina's heart plummeted, and her legs felt loose. Soon people surrounded Drago. They were trying to revive him. It took a couple of minutes for Drago to recover consciousness, but he could not move. Lummy, Rocco, and also Enzo were among the ones who carried Drago out of the stadium. Nobody knew at the time what the extent of his terrible accident was.

CHAPTER NINE

The closing ceremony was canceled. After all the misfortune, Drago had done it. He had won the Horse Master trophy. But he could not be there to receive it. It was sent to Diamond Palace where the only concern at the time was Drago's health. He could not move his legs. After prayers for healing at St. Cesca Cathedral, the prince returned home. His room was going to be his best friend for a long time. It was uncertain if he could walk again.

Queen Constanza devoted her time to provide Drago all the attention and assistance needed. At the servants' lunchroom, the queen gathered everybody and clearly instructed, "Drago's care must be your first priority. Whatever he needs must become your top duty. Every day, every hour, every minute, every second! He will be facing tough physical and emotional challenges. Very difficult days are ahead of him. We must be there for him. We must show him that we care about him. Today he needs all of us. Do you understand?"

"Yes, Your Majesty!" Giorgina, the head housekeeper, said politely with a deep curtsy.

The rest of the staff echoed Giorgina's words and formally greeted the queen.

Queen Constanza bobbed her head and continued, "Bruno went to pick up a curative potion. He should be here any minute. Advise me as soon as he arrives."

"Yes, Queen Constanza," said the head maid. "I'll notify you immediately."

In his room, Drago was in pain. He kept thinking about the accident. He recalled everything about the last race. Images repeated themselves like a scratched disc. Why did he listen to Martina? Maybe if he had taken Dark Knight to the Dressage competition he would have done a better job than White Diamond. Then he would not have had to rush so much in the Show Jumping competition.

Sure, he had a terrible accident, but he never saw what he accomplished. He did not realize that he was the winner of the Horse Master competition. Instead, he only focused on the fall. It was unacceptable to him. He wanted to be perfect and better than everybody else.

At that moment, Drago made a promise to himself: *I will never be on the floor again. I will be on top of everything I touch.*

It seemed as if the accident did not help him to appreciate everything he had achieved. But it helped to nourish his ambition. He decided to use his forced free time to read books, in particular, a red book. *I want to learn about power, control, ruling, and everything to become a master leader. I want the absolute authority to direct the destiny of others,* thought the angry prince.

In her bedroom, Martina was worried about her brother. She wanted to approach him, but she did not know how to do it. She was afraid of his reaction. She knew that Drago was aggressive and irritable.

But one morning, Martina decided to take breakfast to Drago. She slowly walked to the door. She silently opened it and entered the room.

Drago looked at her and said, "Put the tray on the table."

Martina followed his command and added, "How are you feeling?"

"Fine. Don't you see?"

"Do you want me to take you outside? It is a sunny day. You can feel the natural breeze of our garden, and—"

"No! I want to stay here," Drago cut her off.

Martina walked around the room. She did not want to leave. Finally, in the doorway, she said, "By the way, you got a magnificent trophy. It's in the music room."

Martina's words revolved around Drago's head. Regardless of his anger, he was curious about his controversial trophy. He wanted to see it.

Drago sat in his wheelchair and pushed himself into the music room.

There it was, the Horse Master Trophy. It was nicely placed on the fireplace mantel. Drago got close and stared at it. The tragic accident came back to his mind. The fury started invading him. He felt a warm sensation inside. He angrily hit the trophy and threw it against a tall bookcase. He was not only mad for the horse falling, but he also felt weak and helpless tied to a wheelchair.

A loud bang was heard, and there were books scattered all over the place. Drago quickly turned his wheelchair to the piano, pushed the stool away, and started playing some plaintive songs. The redness of his face smoothly disappeared. The piano had always helped him release his compressed energy. It was his escape and relief outlet.

Martina heard the loud noise. She got close to the music room. She pressed her ear to the door, but could hear only music. She slowly opened the door a crack and stuck her head into the room.

Drago was still playing the piano.

Martina was happy to see that her brother was fine. She noticed that the trophy was on the floor, but she did not want to enter the room. She waited for Drago to leave.

Drago finished playing and covered his face with his hands. Heaving a great sigh, he pushed his wheelchair out of the room.

Martina hid behind the door. She quietly entered the room and picked up the trophy. The golden horse prize was in perfect condition.

"What happened, Princess Martina? Are you all right?" said Giorgina in a grim voice as she hurried next to the princess.

"Everything is fine! Please take this trophy to the gallery room. I'm sure my mom has already ordered its display case," requested Martina.

With a lot of patience, Princess Martina piled up the books by category. But a peculiar one caught her attention. It was a yellow book. It smelled old and musty. Yet it carried a spicy scent, a taste that left her stomach growling with curiosity and intrigue.

It looked like a diary. Martina blew the dust off the book. It had the word "joy" and the outline of a key on the front cover. The princess tried to open it, but it was locked. She searched around for the right key, but all the ones she found did not belong to the book. Wonder rolled around in her mind. *What information does the strange journal treasure?* Martina kept the yellow diary, even if she had no key. She stuck it in her bodice and carefully looked to see if Drago was in her way.

It was evident there existed some unusual tension at Diamond Palace. It was hard to deal with Drago's sulky personality. Martina was not indifferent to that feeling. Sometimes she needed some fresh air to recharge her positive batteries.

Almost floating to avoid making any noise, Martina tiptoed

back to her room. She pulled the old book out of her bodice and placed it on her dresser. Where would she find the key? In thoughtful silence, Martina opened up the doors to her balcony and looked out with a sigh.

Suddenly, the princess felt an enormous desire to wander through the streets of Enna Valley without a shadow, even if it meant spraining an ankle in a hole or bumping into a vagrant. She yearned for doing the simple activities that any villager did. She wanted to be free from the yoke of her mother. She picked up ten copper coins and three silver coins. She did not have any gold coins. Still, it was plenty of Brightalian money. She could buy a horse with the ten copper coins or one silver coin.

Martina dug to the bottom of a drawer in her dressing room until she found an old headscarf. It was a present from her nanny. She put it around her head and neck. Then, she pulled on a plain casual dress and snuck out the side gates. That afternoon, Princess Martina wanted to be a real Brightalian.

Martina's first stop was Piano Plaza. There at the center, she observed her dad's statue. "Wow! It's monumental!" she admired. She had never been so close to it. She could not walk her own town. Martina sat on a wood bench and instantly recalled her wooden box. Her bright childhood memories came back. She remembered her birthday trip to the beach. It was a day that she would never forget. She had never used her powers, obeying her mom's obsessive request: *Stay out of magic. It is safer that way.* She had taken some spell classes, but that was pretty much it. Maybe it was time for a big change.

The princess continued her walk along Main Street. Diamond-shaped oil lamps sat at each intersection. She was happy to be out, but sad at the same time and also a bit frightened. Beggars kept approaching her asking for food. The princess just kept her pace.

Martina wound down to Seam Street. She stopped right in front of Casa Victtoria, the main couture house for the royal family. The princess pressed her face against the window. There was Julia, Enzo's mom. Martina perceived her haggard appearance. The lady embroidered a gown. "It must be for my mother!" said Martina with a dimpled smile. Some street workers looked at her. Martina lowered her head and continued her stroll.

A block away from Craft Street, the princess found "the Market". "Interesting place! Worth a visit," she mumbled.

Martina entered the marketplace. She was expecting a splendid place. She had heard that mountains of fresh fruit and vegetables adorned the tables ... that there were bricks of cheese and piles of sausages! But the reality was that the market was just an okay place. In fact, there were a few empty stands. The farming crisis was evident.

One thing was unchanged, the friendly faces of the sellers. The princess was delighted at the kindness of people. Many merchants offered her a little piece to try.

Martina stopped at a cart and bought some bright red apples. She started eating one and continued her slow pace along each aisle. Then she made another stop to get some bread. Right when she was about to leave, she spotted a quaint wood table at the end of the market. It was very different from all the other ones. She walked toward the stand trying to identify what it had. As she got closer, she noticed there was nothing but clear containers full of water.

"Beautiful Martina!" a voice came from behind the table.

Martina removed her old headscarf. "Oh, a stand recognized me!" She moved to the edge of the table trying to see the salesman.

"I've known you since you were born," said the young man as he stood up.

A smile spread across Martina's face. "Finally! You!" The

princess said with excitement. "The stable helper! The Green Lizards warrior! The ghost!" She covered her mouth with her hands. "I mean Fish-face!"

"That's me!" Enzo said proudly, folding his arms. "My name is Enzo Latte."

"Enzo Latte!" repeated Martina. "I've seen you everywhere … at the palace, the horse competition … everywhere!" It seemed like many places to her. "Do you work everywhere?"

Enzo thought for a moment. "Yes, everywhere. But I'm most popular here!" The first part was a lie, but the second one was true. Enzo was a quirky and ingenious guy. Everybody at the market knew and liked him from the first day.

"And you helped my brother when he had the horse accident," Martina followed up. "I remember everything."

"Handsome and attractive! How can somebody forget the King of the Sea?" Enzo posed like a model. He was a strong guy with golden skin from the sun. His straight hair had a chestnut color matching his big brown eyes. He was good looking according to the girls who visited the market.

Martina could not hold back her laughter. She was having fun, and it was not at the palace. "And may I ask what Fish-face … sorry, sorry—" she said, breathing a sigh. "The King of the Sea sells?"

"I sell the greatest variety of fish you could ever find," explained Enzo as he pulled out a big tank from under the table. "By the end of the afternoon, all of these containers must be gone! Every customer who stands right in front of my table must buy a fish, or two, or three—"

This time, they both let out a soft chortle.

"Okay! If that's the requirement for being here, I will buy one, but only one fish," said Martina raising a finger. She started gazing at the tank.

After a little while, Martina spotted the fish, a small betta with vibrant blue colors. At the edges, the fins were pure white like a thin brush had outlined them. But what really caught Martina's attention was the rainbow shading in one of its side fins. It was unique.

"That one! I like that one!" requested Martina.

"Oh nope, nope!" Enzo crossed his arms. "That's my favorite betta fish," he added with a fake cry.

Martina frowned and stated again, "I want that one, the betta fish with the anchor on its fin. Just like the tattoo on your face."

"You're talking about this?" Enzo pointed at his left cheek. "I was born with this mark. Maybe that's why I love the sea so much."

"The sea! I love it too!" Martina got excited.

"Anyways, are you going to buy a fish or not?"

"Yes! I said I want the betta fish," the princess insisted.

"Okay! It's yours, my royal princess! But it is going to cost you more. This tattoo fish is mega expensive. It costs one copper coin."

"Not a problem, I'll pay whatever amount the King of the Sea requests," responded Martina, flirting with the sharp fish seller. She placed two copper coins on top of the cart.

A grin instantly cropped up on Enzo's face. He grabbed a small net and started chasing the betta fish until he caught it. He put it in one of the containers with water and gave it to the princess.

Martina glanced at the small, but beautiful fish. "Tattoo! I will call you Tattoo!"

"Catchy name!" Enzo added.

"And how catchy is King of the Sea?" asked Martina with curiosity to find out how he got that name. She could understand Fish-face, but King of the Sea?

"That is a long story, one that I do not know if I should tell you. Nobody knows it, but me and my fish," said Enzo, waiting for Martina to beg him to reveal his sea story.

"I paid you for the most expensive fish." Martina's face was very serious now. "I demand you tell me the story."

"Whoa! Most expensive fish!" he talked, very thoughtful. "How can I debate that?" agreed Enzo finally, pretending that he had no choice but to narrate his story. "Well, every morning I get up very early and go to the beach."

"Yes, the beach! Can I go with you?"

"Your Highness, don't interrupt. Please!" replied Enzo as he continued his story. "In my fishing boat, I go to the deep, deep sea. Some days the water is very rough, but I battle every big wave. I know the secrets to controlling the brave sea. With my big round net, I swim to the bottom of the ocean. Small, big, round, long, pale, bright, all kinds of fish freely navigate the deep waters. I carefully pick my prospective supply of new fish, and then I swim up to the top. It is not an easy task. Once I reach the tip of my boat, I attach my fishing net to a steel hook, allowing the fish to remain in the water. I place fish by fish into my sophisticated tank, and then I commence my ride back to the shore. That is my tough duty every morning. It takes a lot of courage and strength to go to the deep sea. This is why people call me the King of the Sea."

"Wow, I'm impressed!" responded Martina, looking amazed.

"I said no interruptions, please," restated Enzo.

"I'm so sorry King of the Sea! You may continue," added Martina with a shallow curtsy as if he were a real king.

"The most important part of my morning journey is—"
Martina's eyes widened.

"—that everything that I just told you is not true." Enzo leaned back against the stand.

"*What?*" Martina covered her open mouth.

"This is just my dreamed sea story, my make-believe story to everybody." Enzo paused. "The truth is …"

The princess anxiously waited for an explanation.

"I get the fish from a stream at the back of my house. *The End!*" finished Enzo, looking away from Martina.

Martina gaped at Enzo with confusion. She did not know what to say. She wanted to laugh but found it inappropriate. She finally told Enzo, "Your story is very interesting and creative. But, why did you invent that story? Why don't you tell the truth?"

Enzo gave Martina an embarrassed look and added, "My dad once told me: *Whenever you dream, dream big!*"

Martina's eyes went wide again captivated by the wonderful expression.

"I can't afford a boat. But I still wanted to dream big, so I invented my King of the Sea story."

"But Enzo, I don't think you're getting the right message."

"No, no, no! You didn't know my dad." Enzo put away some of the empty jars. "You must be very busy."

"Well … yes! It's getting late." Martina grabbed her container. "It was a royal pleasure meeting you."

"An honor for me!" The fish salesman continued cleaning his cart. "See ya … soon!" wished Enzo.

"Maybe," added Martina.

"If you come back one day, I promise that I will take you to my secret creek," insisted Enzo, continuing with his packing routine.

"Deal," smiled Martina as she walked away.

"I hope you enjoy your new fish Tutto," called Enzo.

"It's Tattoo!" Martina corrected him.

Martina could not explain why she was in such a good mood.

Enzo was a nice guy, and Tattoo was the last thing Martina imagined buying at a food place. Quick as a wink, her mind got lost in space. Enzo was in her thoughts. He seemed kind and funny too. He made her feel so good even with his crazy stories. *I can have a friend or maybe more than a friend. Am I starting to fall for him? The street boy? Maybe that's a silly idea.*

It was dark, but the oil lamps illuminated the roads in bright violet color. Martina's unique eyes sparkled as much as the stars did in the night sky. There, at the top of the hill, was Diamond Palace also lit in violet. Its rays gradually shimmied up to the moving clouds. Martina was so lost in her thoughts that she barely noticed when she reached Piano Plaza. There, a scene forced her to come right back to earth. A homeless man slept beside one of those radiant light poles. On his flat belly lay a sign that read: *I'm hungry. Please help.* Martina quietly approached the man and raised his grimy blanket to cover his back. She then removed her handkerchief and placed it as a pillow. "Brightalia needs to change ... soon!" assured the princess as a tear rolled down to the rough sidewalk. Next to the man, she left the bread she had bought at the market.

Martina entered the palace and crept up to her room. She placed the clear container next to her secret box. She decided to add a little bit of her magical sand to the bottom of the container for a more natural look. She grasped a handful of sand and let it slide into the water.

"I'll never eat you. You'll be my little pet." Martina talked to the fish. The small betta bubbled inside the container. Then, the princess opened up the doors of her balcony. A full moon loomed in the distance. Staring at the shiny stars, the princess remembered the nice message that Enzo had told her:

Whenever you dream, dream big. She wished she could help her people. She wanted to build houses with fields for farming. She knew it was an ambitious dream knowing that Brightalia could not touch Lusha Land. Still, she wished she could live her dream!

It was close to midnight, but instead of going to bed, Martina tiptoed across to Drago's room. She opened the door slowly. She noticed a messy stack of books on the floor. She walked carefully, so as not to trip over them. She searched for the red book, the one that Drago spent hours studying but refused to show anyone. It was not on the floor. In the long bookcase, she could not find it either. She wondered what the book was about.

On the night table, Martina checked the array of remedies for her brother. Being bound to a wheelchair had also made Drago get close to paper and pencil. Martina spied on some of the drawings. Weird monsters were the consistent theme. A peculiar one caught her eyes. It showed giant creatures tearing down buildings, except for one, a tall and narrow house very different from the architecture of the time. Martina folded the drawing and tossed it down into her nightgown pocket. She then got close to Drago, gently touched his forehead, and whispered in his ear, "You are my brother, and no matter what you do, no matter where you are, I will always love you." Martina headed back to her room, and at her bed, she pleasantly fell asleep. It was a short, but restful night for Martina.

CHAPTER TEN

Day after day, Drago made great progress. After about a month, he was able to hobble around on crutches, still feeling some dull pain from the injury. But soon after that, the potions finally did their job. The prince had fully recovered from the horse accident.

Many believe it was a miracle. For Drago, it was just what needed to happen. His lips never expressed a word of gratitude for all the care and love he received. Drago's room looked like another library. It was impressive the amount of books he had read.

Martina finally got a hold of the book that Drago kept hidden. She was pretty sure her brother had to be learning something good. In gold, the Brightalia coat of arms was on the cover of the heavy book. The princess sat on Drago's bed and carefully opened the book half way – just to realize that the mysterious book was written in Jeslemagian, an ancient language. She recognized most of the letters, but there were some new ones too. She figured it had to be easy to understand the language. Well, it was not!

I wonder how Drago is reading this book. Did he learn

Jeslemagian? Martina kept flipping the pages forward. Page JLIII! Here she saw a familiar name. *Drago? Why is his name on the book?* Martina questioned. The word "Drago" was part of the story on that page.

Straightaway, some loud steps got close to the door. The princess dropped the book on the floor and jumped over the bed just in time to hide in a small space between a corner wall and a long bookcase.

"This palace will change," said Drago with a broad smile as he slammed his bedroom door closed.

Martina swallowed hard. Memories of her childhood flashed into her mind. She remembered when her brother used to chase and scare her. One day he even wore a skull mask. She recalled how the skeletal monster followed her. Martina ran as fast as she could without looking back. She entered the library and skittered under a table. As the shadow of the creature approached her, Martina crawled backward into a space behind a sofa and sneaked out of the room. She rushed to her bedroom and shut the door right on the nose of the black creature. She was definitely glad those days were gone.

Drago picked up the book and flopped down into his bed. "How did you get to the floor?"

Martina's heart fluttered. *Now what?* She made her greatest effort to think straight. Her eyes drifted to Drago and then to her feet. She noticed a violet key between her shoes. She did not want to move to avoid making any noise. She almost did not want to breathe.

Just then, a knock came at the door. "Prince Drago! Dinner is almost ready. Their Majesties will be waiting for you." It was the mild voice of Giorgina.

"Dinner! Got it!" responded Drago. He did not open the door. He just continued reading the red book.

Martina was about to die at the corner wall. How would she leave the room without her brother noticing? She needed some help. For the first time, she thought her powers could come in handy. She closed her eyes and magically summoned a gust of sand that smashed some pictures hanging inside Drago's dressing room. The frames collapsed to the floor and shattered glass spread all over the room.

Drago rushed to check the mess and closed the windows. He had a befuddled look on his face.

Martina did not waste a second to escape and sprinted across to her bedroom. She closed the door behind her and slid down to the floor. She rested her head against the door and breathed out in relief. "Magic can actually be good!" she told herself.

The princess opened her hand and looked at the violet key she had found in Drago's room. Immediately, a memory struck her. She recalled the old yellow diary she found in the music room. It had a sketch of a key and the word "joy" on its front cover. The book was still on her desk under the wooden box. She carefully placed the key over the outline. The violet key matched the shape to perfection.

The princess was ready to unlock the secret book. She inserted the key in the opening and slowly turned the key to the right. A click was heard and the diary opened by itself.

The book lifted into the air flipping its pages back and forth. It then landed back on Martina's hands.

Opened on the first page, the yellow journal was handwritten but fully readable. Black ink contoured every letter. The diary contained some poetry as well.

Martina started reading the book as though she were looking for some answers. But a question came sooner than an answer. The diary started changing its color. It completely turned red. The word on its cover became "caution".

How is that possible? Where does the journal come from? the princess wondered. *Is the color giving me a message about Drago's red book?* Martina's head turned into a cloud of questions. She stared at the journal one last time, but she had to go down for dinner.

The princess was the last one to arrive at the turquoise dining salon. She quickly got to her chair.

King Alessio started talking. "Tomorrow starts the Annual Confederation Meeting at the Castella Kingdom. Your mother and I must attend."

"Our presence is very important this time. New Castella settlements have usurped a large portion of the disputed territory," added Queen Constanza.

"You mean Lusha Land?" asked Drago, stirring his stew.

"Yes, Drago," King Alessio nodded. The pressing tension to find a resolution to the Lusha Land conflict escalated after we asked Castella to withdraw their settlers. We must be there. We can't take the risk of losing a valuable land." This time, the king did not seem too hungry. Most of his pork was untouched. "We want to reach an agreement. Our kingdom is trying to prevent a war."

"A war!" repeated Martina.

"Don't worry about it yet. I'm sure we will get to a peaceful resolution." King Alessio grabbed the apple from the roasted pig's mouth. "I must admit it's time to sign the agreement even if it entails giving up most of the land."

"Why give away land? Don't do that, Father!" complained Drago. He pushed his bowl to the side. "In fact, all the land should be for Brightalia. We need it more than them!"

"We must end the long struggling years of debates and get

some land," King Alessio countered. His face showed discontent at Drago's words.

Queen Constanza cleared her throat to get her husband's attention. "Not everything is bad news." She managed a vague smile. "Our last crop was saved."

"Yes, but soon it won't be enough to feed our entire kingdom." King Alessio looked very concerned. So much that he skipped his favorite part of the meal, dessert.

Queen Constanza's mind had already traveled to all the galas that she was going to attend at the Castella Confederation Meeting. "The balls will be spectacular, and ... of course, your dad will work out the best resolution to benefit our people ... as he always does," she said in snatches. The queen's bundle of suitcases with all her sparkling gowns were packed and ready to go at the front doors. "I can't wait to leave tomorrow!"

"I will miss you so much!" expressed Martina as she pushed her chair close to the queen and wrapped her mother's arm.

"Everything will be all right," responded Queen Constanza, stroking Martina's head. "Your hair is crispy."

"It's fine, Mother. Just wavy."

"Dante! Do me a favor," requested King Alessio.

The head butler walked toward the king. "Yes, Your Majesty," responded Dante with a bow.

"Please order some coffee to the music room," nodded the king. "I feel it will be a long trip," he then mumbled, stretching his neck.

"Certainly," said Dante, going out the side door and taking the staircase down to the kitchens.

The family joined together in the music room. King Alessio stood at the window. Then, he began to pace the room fretfully until a kitchen maid entered with the coffee cart.

"I hope we can keep cultivating these great shrubs," said the king as Giorgina handed him a cup of coffee. He went to his usual blue armchair.

That evening, Drago did not play the piano as usual. He decided to sit beside his dad. He wanted to learn more about the Lusha Land boundary controversy. King Alessio filled in his son with information as Drago listened carefully.

Queen Constanza did not miss the chance to share time with her daughter. "Come with me," said Queen Constanza.

"What is it, Mother?" asked Martina.

"You'll see," responded Queen Constanza as she held Martina by the hand.

The queen and daughter crossed the main blue hallway and walked together to the east wing of the palace. It was the business side of the building where the Council's hall, Diamond Office, audience chamber, and throne room were.

"Is it important?" asked the princess.

"It is necessary. I will show you the unique view of the east tower," Queen Constanza said fondly.

"Great!" Martina gave a smiley look. "I've seen the secret view of the west tower. Mercy showed it to me when I was a young girl," added Martina.

"The views are not secret. They are just unique," gently clarified the queen.

The spiral stairs were very narrow and ended up in a small room. Tall rectangular windows allowed the sunlight to filter inside the tower.

Queen Constanza walked to a crystal door that opened up to the outside balcony. There, Martina saw the end of Enna Valley and the beginning of the long snaky roadway that led to the beach.

"*Wow!* This is truly my favorite view!" said Martina with unblinking eyes. "I want to go back to the beach."

"Martina, here is the opposite end of Brightalia," said the queen with brooding eyes. The west view is Lusha Land, and the east view here is the road to Amo Island."

Martina listened with concern.

"If both ends are at peace, then our kingdom is happy and full of bright light," explained the queen. She turned and looked at her daughter warily. "Flames arriving at one of the unique views of the palace can mark the end of our kingdom. That is the true concealed secret of the views."

Martina frowned. "Let me see if I understand you. Brightalia can be consumed by a fire that will start at Lusha or Amo Island?"

"Yes, the ancient wizards of Brightalia made that prediction centuries ago." The queen moved closer to her daughter. "Honey, this is why I want you to stay away from magic. I know you have the power to control sand. But it can get very complicated here in Brightalia if you try to help."

"I will never harm anyone!" expressed Martina. She wished her mom would see her magic differently.

"I know dear, but that doesn't grant you safety." Queen Constanza clasped Martina's shoulder and looked straight into her eyes. "Promise me that you won't use your powers or leave the palace while we're away."

"Please, Mother! Don't ask me that," she said in a squeaky voice.

"Do it, please!" The queen hugged Martina. "I just want to protect you."

"I understand, but …!" Martina remained silent for a moment until finally, she yielded, "I promise!" She put her arms around her mom.

CHAPTER ELEVEN

Very early the next morning, King Alessio and Queen Constanza were ready to leave for the kingdom of Castella. The royal carriage was at the main courtyard awaiting the king and queen. Drago and Martina were also at the door to say goodbye to their parents.

"I heard our parents talking about you having some kind of strange, magical powers," whispered Drago in his sister's ear.

"I wish. I would make you a truly handsome prince!" laughed Martina. "You must have been dreaming!"

"Just tell me. Is it true?" Drago gritted his teeth, staring at Martina.

"Yes, I can read the future, and my scrying ball tells me that you're a tardy away to being suspended." The princess winked at Drago.

"How do you know?" Drago looked surprised.

"I'm a wicked witch!" said Martina in a ghostly voice.

"You really sound creepy!"

"And I'm not acting at all," Martina turned around and stood next to one of the guards, away from Drago.

The king and queen got to the door wearing elegant formal

attire and their royal crowns. The precious stones on Queen Constanza's gown were the real standout of her majestic outfit. Her glamour could not stay behind.

Guards lined up from the palace main doors all the way out of to the front gates. Bruno held the door open for the king and queen to enter the JOR.

King Alessio kissed Martina on her cheek. Martina hugged her dad and buried her head in the king's chest.

The princess deeply felt the love of her dad. "Please come back soon," wept Martina. For some inexplicable reason, she felt she did not want her parents to leave this time.

"It's only a few days, my dearest daughter," responded the king.

"Be good my son and take care of your sister," King Alessio advised Drago, hugging his son tight.

"Take care of yourself too," Queen Constanza added, giving Drago a kiss.

"Have a good trip," responded Drago, waving his hand.

"Mother," cried Martina. Her heart began to palpitate faster than usual. The princess encircled her arms around the queen with warm love.

Queen Constanza gently brushed away Martina's tears. She looked straight at Martina's wet eyes and said with a broken voice, "I love you, my daughter. I'll see you pretty soon." The queen warmed Martina's face with her soft hands.

Ringing the main courtyard, the royal carriage soon disappeared passing the stunning front gates of Diamond Palace. The flashy coach headed straight to the Brightalia railroad station for the king and queen to board the train to Castella.

The Annual Confederation meeting commenced at noon with a welcoming ceremony. There was a general gathering in the afternoon followed by a formal dinner and a gala reception that night.

The King and Queen of Castella presided over all the events. Strict rules and security measures were established for each occasion. There were soldiers in every corner, something that King Alessio and Queen Constanza found uncomfortable and unnecessary.

The following couple of days were filled with tight agendas outlining all the scheduled meetings and activities. In general, the conference went well despite the long hours of intense debates. Brightalia gained some good ground regarding the Lusha Land problem. Castella agreed to withdraw their settlers from the claimed territory back to their kingdom. However, there were still some minor boundary issues that needed to be resolved before signing the agreement.

A second assembly between the two neighboring kingdoms, Brightalia and Castella, was going to take place in a couple of months. King Alessio and Queen Constanza were mostly satisfied with the outcomes of the Confederation meeting.

Before boarding the train to Brightalia, King Alessio told Queen Constanza, "I must tell you something, I hope you will support."

The queen drifted her wide eyes to her husband. "What could that be?"

"I love you very much."

The queen blushed like a teenager. "You have all my support. Love you too!"

King Alessio hugged his wife with deep affection as they boarded the Castella train to return home.

Martina was very anxious about the arrival of her parents. The princess noticed that her diary had not switched back to yellow. It remained red, and it still displayed the word "caution" on the cover. Martina's heart beat fast again. She promptly opened the book and read the last lines.

As nature takes the stage,
Uncertain is the ride,
Winning for the light,
Or being trapped in utter darkness.

No one knows, nobody expects
As far as the West,
As close to the East,
Suddenly everything seems so far.

For in this darkness,
There is something to find.
Run, run, run,
Hope is in the sand,
For no rocks about to fall,
For no tracks about to crash.

Inside this dark is nothing,
Yet everything can still change.

She could not get a clear idea about the message. Yet she got concerned at seeing the word sand in the poem. She also puzzled over the color and word of the diary, but she was too excited to give it too much thought. One thing Martina was sure about. She had promised her mom not to use her powers. Martina instructed Donato, the main cook, to prepare her parents' favorite meals, all types of desserts, fruits, and a special cake welcoming the king and queen. "I want to give them a nice surprise," said Martina with a radiant look.

"Everything will be ready for the royal couple," responded Donato with a friendly voice. He kept the kitchens busy that evening.

Impatiently, Martina got to her bedroom. Looking out the balcony, she tried to spot the royal coach. "It seems like the train is delayed!" The princess bit at her lip in worry. Martina ambled across the room and gazed at the magical diary again. Bright red was still its color! She did not want to open the book again. Martina decided to go to the turquoise dining salon and add personal touches to the table: candle stands made of sand.

It was getting late, and regardless of her effort, Martina could not avoid overthinking about the last poem. Its words resonated with her and kept her head whirling.

...

Run, run, run,
Hope is in the sand

...

But right away, she heard the fuming wheels of the royal carriage. Martina flew downstairs to open the door. In a matter of seconds, Drago and Mercy arrived at the main courtyard. The JOR flashed past the main gates and abruptly halted its progress just a couple feet away from the royal siblings. Bruno got out of the coach in one spring. He had a haunted look as if he had just come out of a horror house. The princess took a hesitant step forward, but she could not reach the coach, as Mercy pulled her back. "Wait, my princess."

"Where are my parents?" asked Drago who jerked his head

inside the passenger window and stared at the empty seats.

"Your Highness!" The coachman removed his cap and bent his head. "I regret to inform you that there has been an accident," briefed Bruno. His voice was trembling.

"That's not true!" Martina let out a squeal.

Mercy grabbed Martina by her shoulders. "Calm down, my princess. I'm sure Their Majesties are fine," she whispered in Martina's ear. The nanny observed Bruno's blue uniform. It was covered with dust from the hectic ride. The horses were pretty lathered up and bathed in sweat. Their noisy sniffing was non-stop. If a lake had been in front of them, it was almost sure they would have gulped it down to the last drop.

"What happened?" said Drago with a blank gaze.

"The Brightalia terminal officials alerted me that the train had crashed," explained the loyal coachman. "The entire mishap area is in flames."

"Has someone located the royal carriage of the train?" asked Drago, his voice grim.

"Not yet." Bruno took a deep breath. "I decided it was better to come back rather fast even if I could only tell you …" His voice faltered. "That the royal couple is missing."

Martina gasped in sorrow at the painful news. She fell down in tears. "Please Drago, find our parents and bring them home!" sobbed Martina, gripping her brother's shirt.

"I will, Martina. I promise!" Drago hugged his sister with deep affection. "I will not stop… I will not sleep until I see them again." Tears slipped out of the prince's eyes.

Martina felt great support from her brother. She was confident that he would do everything possible to save their parents. She trusted Drago. "I know you'll rescue them," said Martina, weeping. "I know you will!"

For a few minutes that seemed to last longer than an hour, the two siblings let their grief surface, keeping their arms around each other.

"I must go now," Drago finally said, kissing his sister's forehead and then leading her to Mercy. "Stay with her," Drago instructed the nanny. Promptly, the prince hurried inside the palace, wiping the tears from his cheeks.

The princess sat at the turquoise dining salon and cried for hours. There was a hurricane of feelings inside of her. She knew Drago had to take the lead in the arduous quest for the royal couple. Yet she wished her brother could be with her. At the mournful feeling of not knowing about her parents, the princess felt protected next to her brother.

Mercy tried to comfort her, but Martina was in painful denial. "Let me take you to your room, Your Highness." Mercy helped the princess get up from the king's dining chair.

Right away, Prince Drago hopped on a horse ready to ride straight for the station. But as the councilors hurriedly arrived at the palace, Lady Zirry, Councilor of Health, stopped him. "Your Highness! You should go inside."

"No! I must get to the train station to find out about my parents."

"We already have some news," Lady Zirry said quickly. She wore a scarlet robe. Tall and thin, the councilor had her ashen hair drawn back into her habitual bun. "Please! Let's work together to rescue Their Majesties."

Prince Drago hesitated for about a quarter of a minute. Then he got off the horse and in desperate haste, entered the Council's hall. Lady Zirry showed at the door right behind the prince. Drago quickly reached his dad's chair. But he could not even touch it. Instead, he took a few steps to the side. He hummed his throat clear and promptly got straight to the point, "Who knows any details about the train accident?"

"Your Highness!" The Emissary to Foreign Affairs raised a hand. He had just come back from the Brightalia railroad station. "It's my understanding that the train derailed and caught fire," explained Lord Ferro with a brisk voice. His black wig was always perfectly combed to the back, except for that night. Strands of hair going in all directions covered his shiny forehead.

Drago turned to the emissary. "What caused the accident?" asked the prince, observing the disheveled appearance of Lord Ferro.

"The train collided with boulders that had fallen on the line. The impact caused the carriage to break in two, and cars ended up scattered all over the area," continued Lord Ferro.

Drago saw how all eyes stared at him. "Was the accident on Brightalia territory?" the prince managed to ask while realizing that everybody was waiting to follow his commands. For the first time, he was representing his dad, and he had become the head of the rescue operation, one he wanted to be successful at. It was time to start practicing his leadership skills.

"No, Your Highness," a stumbling voice responded. "The train derailed before passing the culvert near the Brightalia border," added Lord Campo. The Emissary to Land Resources was very fond of the king. His face could not hide his concern and sadness.

"A couple of hours away. We must act now and quickly," Prince Drago emphasized with a firm voice. "Is the Chief of Army here?" Drago scanned faces, looking for General Althar.

"Waiting for your orders," responded the general from the back. "Regiments are ready to depart at the main command center."

"What's the fastest way?"

It was again Lord Campo who answered the prince's question. "Through the west hills bordering Lusha, Your Highness! Even though that is not the safest way, crossing across the main farmlands will take twice as long. The terrain is very rocky mainly at the crest, but it's not impossible to make it through."

Prince Drago did not take long to make up his mind. "Hit the high grounds." His eyes flicked to the general. "Your task is exclusively to find the king and queen—" Drago paused and strode to the wall where the portrait of King Alessio hung. "Alive," he added in a low voice.

There was a tearful silence in the entire hall. Councilors looked at each other with doleful faces. None articulated a word.

Prince Drago took a determined breath and walked back next to his dad's chair, resting one arm on the well-padded back. Then he ordered, "I don't want any delays searching for other useless stuff. As cruel as it may sound, you're only there to save my parents. Don't waste any time. Are we clear?"

"Yes, Your Highness," responded Althar with extreme hesitation and an affirmative military salute, making it quite confusing to understand if he was in agreement or disagreement with the prince.

Drago snapped his fingers loudly. "What are you waiting for? Sitting here costs us time we don't have to spare. Let's give those horses a training exercise."

Althar got to the tall double doors in one single hop. But with the same impulse, he turned back inside. "Can I make a request?"

"What is it, General?"

"Could Lord Campo join my elite squad? He knows the area better than anybody around here." Althar exited the room again.

"Sure thing!" The prince signaled Lord Campo to follow behind the general. He was able to catch Campo's round eyes through his thick glasses. Drago also got out of the room, but took the opposite doors leading toward the Diamond Office.

The clock kept ticking and Lord Ferro had just finished briefing Martina about the details of the accident. When he left the princess's bedroom, the first thing that came to Martina's mind was the last poem in her diary. She picked up the journal again. This time, she carefully read most of the pages. *How did I miss it?* The magical diary was describing her life as it happened. The last poem, as well as the color and word on the cover, were all warnings of the accident. She felt as if the boulders had fallen on top of her head. *It's my fault. I could have prevented the crash. Now I get it,* she cried. The charmed book had written the poem to advise Martina to take action. Unfortunately, she did not understand the message. She was just starting to understand the journal. *The diary was telling me to use my sand to stop the rocks, to shield the way and avoid the crash!* Martina read with sad eyes:

...

Run, run, run,
Hope is in the sand,
For no rocks about to fall,
For no tracks about to crash.

...

Martina recalled she had promised her mom she was not going to leave the palace or use her powers while they were away. Could she have broken her promise and saved the royal couple? It was too late to take the blame, but she could not avoid feeling guilty. The painful thoughts kept revolving in her head hour after hour.

Past midnight, a corner of the diary darkened. Martina fixed her eyes at the weird journal. The color continued spreading along the cover until the whole book had turned black. Martina blanched at the color. Her heart plummeted. She did not have strength to open the book this time. Instead, she went looking for Drago. The door of the Diamond Office was ajar, and Martina stepped inside. There she found him, and there she heard some awaited words.

"The royal couple has been located in the disaster area," announced Lord Campo who was barely recognizable. His body was ashen, and his smell was nasty. And that was being conservative.

Drago dropped a pen from his hand and stood. His eyes glowed like fireflies. "And ... are they alive?"

CHAPTER TWELVE

Mercy entered the Diamond Office looking for Martina. Giorgina followed behind her with a coffee tray. The nanny stopped suddenly and raised a hand to Giorgina to remain at the door when she saw the dreadful look of the princess.

"Are my parents alive?" repeated Prince Drago in a demanding tone.

Martina pressed her diary against her chest. She felt how Mercy's warm hands touched the back of her shoulders.

Lord Campo removed his dirty glasses and glanced at Martina, then Drago. "The royal carriage of the train was badly hit. I must say it was pretty much destroyed. It took us a while to spot it. It was General Althar who identified one of the outside walls of the coach. It still had part of the Brightalia coat of arms—"

"Campo!" Drago cut him off, raising his voice. "Leave the details for later and tell me about my parents."

Everybody eyed the Emissary to Land Resources anxiously. The coffee cups clinked as the tray almost slid out of Giorgina's hands.

Lord Campo bent his head and gulped, "I never imagined having to deliver this news." His voice faded away as he tried to hold back his tears. "I'm deeply sorry to inform you that Their Majesties did not survive the accident." He sighed and then went on, "King Alessio was a great man, and I will never forget the queen's beautiful smile. I was privileged to have served the royal couple for twenty years." Tears came to his eyes.

"I want to see my mom and dad," wailed the princess. Martina could not believe her parents would never come back. Mercy took Martina to a chair. Drago knelt in front of his sister and held her close in his arms.

Lord Campo asked Mercy and Giorgina to leave the room and give some time alone to the siblings.

"I have failed," sobbed Drago. "I couldn't save them."

Martina caught her breath for a moment. "It was not your fault. You did what you had to do."

Hours passed without them noticing. Eventually, Drago stood, and jutting out his chin, he said, "I have a lot of work to do now. I better keep moving." The prince blew a kiss to Martina and departed from the room rather quickly.

Martina was still digesting the painful news. She headed to her bedroom, and at her writing desk, she opened her black diary. The princess read the most beautiful, but at the same time, the saddest lines of her magical book. The words were very clear this time and somehow helped to alleviate her grief.

Embrace the good memories,
Keep them in your mind,
For your heart is broken,
The love is still inside.

Today is a sad day,
Tomorrow can turn gray,
But for all the strength you need,
We will always be there.

Deep inside your soul,
Or up the moving clouds,
Our voices you'll hear,
In every time of doubt.

You will not be alone,
You will never have to fear,
That for every minute,
And in every single day,
Remember, remember,
In your heart is where we'll stay!

Martina gathered her diary and slowly walked to the queen's bedroom. "How can I fill this empty space?" cried the princess. She lay on the queen's bed and squeezed hard on the silky sheets. More tears cascaded from Martina's eyes. The princess opened her black book again. She thought she was living a nightmare. She wanted to wake up. Martina tried to empty her tormented mind, but memories kept surfacing. She could not control the tears running down her cheeks and dripping onto the poem.

Mercy prepared a tasty herbal tea for the princess.

"Mercy!" sobbed Martina as the kind maid entered the bedroom.

"I brought you some tea, my princess," said the nanny. She set the tray down and handed the princess the cup of hot tea.

Martina took a couple of sips and rested her head on Mercy's shoulder.

Mercy stayed with the princess until she fell asleep hugging her diary.

The next morning, Martina dressed in a long black tunic with a violet armband. Her hair was pulled back into a bun. She looked at the balcony and saw how everybody was slowly arriving at Piano Plaza.

Villagers and farmers were all leaving flowers around King Alessio's statue. Handcrafted gifts for the royal siblings were also deposited at the plaza. She was able to notice Enzo and his mom as they were in line to set down their flower bouquet.

Martina felt the affection everybody at Brightalia had for the royal couple. Deep in her heart, Martina was thankful for all the warm support. The princess observed the plaza, but she did not want to go down. It was too devastating for her.

Drago paced along the main hallway toward the Council's hall. He stepped inside the room and gazed at the audience. The room was packed with advisors and dignitaries. The prince wore a formal black robe with a purple collar.

All councilors were dressed in black robes as well. They all stood muttering about the terrible news.

This time, Drago walked straight to his dad's chair. "By now, I'm sure you are all aware that King Alessio and Queen Constanza will not be with us anymore," started Drago with a fixed look. "Any updates on their bodies' arrival?

"Bruno left very early this morning in the royal carriage," explained Lord Ferro. His black wig was already in place, as usual, well combed to the back.

Drago looked at his pocket watch. "How long for him to come back?" asked Drago, stretching his neck sideways.

"Most of the fires have been put out, but it's still risky to enter the red area," Lord Ferro went on. "Bruno will station close to the Brightalia border."

Drago rose from the chair and swaggered to a window. "Who is in charge of transporting the bodies to the JOR?" asked Drago, looking outside.

"The elite squad, Your Highness," Lord Campo responded this time. "They have taken all precautions to smoothly transport the stretchers to the meeting location," added the Emissary to Land Resources.

With hands together behind his back, Drago strutted around the room. "Any Brightalian survivors?" asked the prince with a dry smile.

"Unfortunately, none so far," said Lord Ferro in a quavering voice. "All crew members died."

"Your Highness, I must add—" A face showed up at the doors.

"Come inside, General," interrupted Drago.

General Althar got to the front of the room with his typical military salute.

Prince Drago shook his head. "Any additional details about Their Majesties?" said Drago with a bleak look.

"Yes! A search party is also on the way to the accident location. Their mission is to salvage any belongings of King Alessio and the queen," explained General Althar.

"And who authorized a search party?" asked Drago, raising his voice almost to a shout.

"It is the protocol, Your Highness, in any disaster event," replied the general with a confused look.

"Any other update?" inquired Drago.

"Yes! A second regiment left this morning to recover our citizens' bodies. The Ambassador from Castella, Lord Falco, will arrive at noon. His kingdom has offered to help in our rescue operation. They know the impacted area extremely well," continued General Althar.

"And who says we need help?" Drago spat. "His presence here is not welcome." The prince gave General Althar a sardonic look, walking out of the Council's hall. "Assembly dismissed!" shouted Drago.

Lord Porto, one of the senior councilors, followed close behind. "Prince Drago, I just want to let you know that I'm already coordinating the memorial service and village feast," said Lord Porto with a low voice.

"There will be no feast this time," answered Drago as he continued making his way to the throne room.

"Your Highness, a funeral feast is traditional in our kingdom. I know our citizens would like to offer you and your sister their sincere condolences. King Alessio and Queen Constanza gained the love and respect of all their people," insisted the councilor.

Drago stopped suddenly and turned back. He stretched his neck to the side and looked at Lord Porto with hard eyes. "I said there will *not* be a feast," restated Drago slowly. "I don't need the pity of anybody. Plan a private memorial service for the morning. Very early in the morning! Do I make myself clear?" commanded Drago.

"Your words are my orders," responded Lord Porto.

Martina did not want to enter the Council's hall. But at the corridor, she overheard a conversation between Lord Porto and Lord Campo expressing concern about Drago's attitude that day. They claimed the prince was acting different, quite mad. Martina wondered what was happening to Drago. She hoped he was just stressed out. Now the princess had nobody else but her brother.

Martina hurried to catch up with the senior councilor as he was leaving. "Lord Porto," she called.

"Princess Martina, I am deeply sorry for your loss," said Lord

Porto with a kind voice.

"Thank you! They are now enjoying the crowns of life," responded the princess.

"How can I help, Your Highness?" asked the councilor.

Martina looked around. "I need a favor. Please advise the bishop to preside at the memorial service," said Martina with a soft voice.

"Certainly!" assured Lord Porto, shaking his head.

"Your Highness," stopped General Althar as he saw the princess. He removed his cap. "Words cannot express my sorrow."

Martina lowered her head. Uncontrollable tears slipped from her glowing eyes again.

"The crowns have been recovered," added General Althar.

"What else has been salvaged?" inquired the princess, wiping away her tears.

"Not much! Prince Drago ordered the search party to return this afternoon," responded Arthar, rubbing his forehead with concern.

"It has been difficult to deal with Prince Drago," added Lord Porto.

"The last two days have been very stressful for all of us," justified Martina.

"Yes, that's very true," concluded Lord Porto. "We hope tomorrow will be a better day."

CHAPTER THIRTEEN

E arly at dawn, the memorial service was held. Prince Drago wore his royal black robe. Just as he requested, the funeral was private and very solemn. Only those closest to the royal family attended.

Just as Martina wished, the Bishop for Brightalia conducted the ceremony. The princess dressed in a black gown with her royal violet sash. A black veil covered her beautiful, but sad face.

Back at Diamond Palace, Martina saw how the two crowns were being prepared for display in the gallery room. She gently touched them. Martina looked at the big oleo painting of the royal couple and said, "You will always be in my heart as well." She recalled the last poem in her diary. She hoped time would help things get better at home.

The princess spent most of her days pleading with Drago to let her participate in the kingdom's activities. But her brother never did.

As the weeks went by, Drago was more distant, even indifferent toward Martina. His angry mood only got worse. Each day, it became more evident that he was desperate to rule and be the new king of Brightalia. Most councilors were in disagreement with him. They claimed he was too young to rule, but the prince roundly opposed to all attempts by the Royal Council to appoint a regent. Drago was hungry for power.

"Where is the crown?" asked Drago as he gave the final orders for coronation day.

The sad memories of the train accident were still vivid in the minds of the Brightalians. But Prince Drago only observed four weeks of mourning following the funeral procession of King Alessio and Queen Constanza. It was the minimum time required according to the kingdom's rules and customs.

Drago's intentions were simple and clear: to get to the throne.

"Here it is, Your Highness," said the Emissary to Internal Affairs, entering the gallery room.

Drago had ordered a new opulent crown, breaking the family tradition of wearing his dad's crown. "Just as the doctor ordered," giggled Drago, holding up the huge crown. The unique piece of art had an unusual hexagonal shape instead of the traditional round one. It was made of platinum and decorated with more than four thousand diamonds. It contained several precious stones, among them sapphires and emeralds. The centerpiece was a 120-carat ruby, which was deemed without equal in the world.

"The ceremony will start promptly at nine o'clock," informed Lord Porto with a plain look.

"Smile, Porto! It is coronation day. Today I'll become the absolute ruler of the Kingdom of Brightalia," said Drago with a sly look.

The prince handed Lord Porto the guest list.

"Make sure our head guard gets his eyes on the list. I don't want any unwelcome villagers to infiltrate our premises asking for a weird petition for their uncles," advised Drago, turning his back on the emissary and striding down to the main hallway.

Lord Porto checked the aristocratic list and walked out of the gallery room, but in the opposite direction. Only the noble families from Brightalia received invitations, as well as a select group of wealthy and influential people from the neighboring Kingdom of Castella. Every guest had to observe a strict dress code.

Drago was the first one to enter the main ballroom. He double-checked that the crown and throne were in place. The future king wore a black tailcoat with matching trousers that fitted nicely around his waist. His black cloak was embroidered in white gold. He was ready to start the show.

Drago formally greeted the distinguished guests at the reception hall. The Emissary to Land Resources was one of the first guests to arrive.

"Let me congratulate you in advance," said Lord Campo with a bow.

"Thank you! Today a new line begins to define the future of Brightalia," philosophized Drago, smiling.

The line of noble and affluent dignitaries was not too long. Soon Drago entered the main ballroom.

As the St. Cesca Cathedral's bells rang the ninth hour of the day, the Bishop of Brightalia stood up followed by all the audience.

Diamond Palace was about to witness the coronation of the forty-ninth King of Brightalia.

The bishop started with a prayer for the kingdom and its

117

people. Then lowering his head, the senior priest closed his eyes and said a silent prayer. He paused for a brief moment.

There was a serene silence in the room.

The bishop raised his head and continued with the ceremony. "Is Your Majesty willing to take the Oath?" the bishop recited.

"I am willing," answered Drago, holding the Sovereignty Book of State.

"Will you promise and swear to govern the people of Brightalia according to their respective laws and customs?"

"Yes, I promise," said Drago, raising his right arm.

"Will you do the utmost within your power to maintain the peace and welfare of Brightalia, its lands, and its people?"

"Yes, I will," responded Drago, bending his head down to the bishop.

The bishop took the new crown and paused again.

Drago rolled up his eyes. There was a long tense silence.

The senior priest moved slowly with hesitation.

Drago kept waiting. His neck started to hurt.

Finally, the bishop placed the heavy crown on the head of the new king.

Drago pressed it down as it tilted slightly to the side. He proceeded to sit on the throne.

Usually, a family member bore the honor of handing the orb and scepter to the new monarch. It would have been Martina's turn to participate in the ceremony. But Drago had previously appointed General Althar to do the honor. Martina just stood at a corner of the room, unnoticed by the senior priest.

The Chief of Army paraded through the ballroom as if he were in a military event.

"Holy cannoli! What is the general doing?" muttered the king under his breath.

Extending his arms, Drago received the orb and scepter,

offering General Althar a fake smile.

The bishop gave King Drago a confused look. He was expecting Martina to do the honor.

Drago nodded with wide eyes.

The bishop cleared his throat and looked at the Sovereignty Book of State. "On the ninth hour of this day, I name you, Drago I, ruler of the Kingdom of Brightalia," intoned the bishop with a solemn voice.

King Drago arose out of the throne and raised the orb and scepter.

As the royal guests cheered, the new king showed the holy items across the room, gloating over his inherited crown. The main ballroom was not large enough to accommodate Drago's monstrous ego. He was ready to change the history of the kingdom.

Breaking the first tradition, King Drago did not have the courtesy to go out the main balcony and greet his people. The celebration was very formal, but it lacked the warm hospitality and glamorous decoration of Queen Constanza. The event did not last too long. It was over after the gala dinner.

Early the following morning, the councilors were in their hall. In black robes, they clustered around the king's chair, chatting and speculating about the destiny of the kingdom. The first assembly of King Drago was about to begin. Drago reached the Council's hall and opened the tall heavy doors.

All councilors rushed to their seats. Princess Martina was entitled to attend, but Drago did not allow her to be there.

"This is a new day, a day of change," said King Drago, walking straight to the royal chair.

Without any formal welcoming, he started his address. "I've

prepared for this moment. I've waited for this opportunity. And the time is finally now. The time to share my doctrine. The time to possess absolute control. The time to impose powerful reforms. The time to recover our lands. The time..." King Drago raised his authoritarian voice as he performed his initial speech. One that nobody expected, but one that everybody got to hear for the next two hours.

CHAPTER FOURTEEN

Infringing the law seemed to be Drago's new legacy. He was determined to impose a new doctrine, a new way of ruling a kingdom.

At the Diamond Office, King Drago held a private meeting with Lord Abewell.

"I need to have absolute control of the distribution of food," said the king, sitting in his chair and moving a pen between his fingers.

"Your Majesty, to my knowledge, the law establishes that—" tried to explain the Commerce and Agriculture Councilor.

"I did not ask you about the law," interrupted the king. Drago rose and banged the royal desk with his fist. "Let me be more specific." He sat down again and lowered his shouting voice. "I need a food storage and distribution center. Find a large building!"

The councilor remained thoughtful. "We don't have such a place," responded Lord Abewell with a small voice. The councilor wiped the sweat off his almost bald head.

"I have it! Why didn't I think about it before? I'm a genius!" said King Drago with a sarcastic look.

Lord Abewell's eyes got round.

"The Market!" announced the king.

"The Market!" repeated Lord Abewell, giving a sudden jerk of his head. His jaw dropped without him even noticing. "Your Majesty," the councilor sighed. "I thought you meant an empty building. You know the Market is the only location where our farmers sell their cultivated products, the place where our villagers buy their food." Abewell cleaned his sweat off again.

"Exactly! It's the perfect place to become a distribution center." Drago rubbed his chin, grinning. King Drago did not care about the kingdom's economy. He was focused on his arbitrary plan, one that according to him would solve the food scarcity problem.

"Every rancher, every farmer, and even the poorest peasant will take his entire production and turn it into the kingdom authorities at the Market," said King Drago with an arrogant voice. He walked to a window and looked out to the main courtyard.

Lord Abewell looked flustered. "Your Majesty, if I may ask: Why? What are you trying to achieve?"

"Power and recognition! Everybody will receive the same amount of food. Nobody will be hungry anymore. Brightalians will love me. And I will control every piece of bread in this town. Is that clear enough?" Drago smiled and continued admiring the courtyard view.

"It's clear." The councilor frowned and shook his head in disagreement. "Who will be in charge of the process?"

"That will be your new job," King Drago responded flatly. He turned around and narrowed his eyes at the councilor.

"With all due respect, Your Majesty, I don't see how this new center will benefit our people. I think you're making a terrible mistake," said Lord Abewell with a trembling voice. The councilor grabbed a glass and took a sip of water.

"Enough with the questioning! Even the freedom to make my own mistakes is what I want," shouted King Drago, raising his hand as though to strike his desk. "Let me make myself clear, and I mean as clear as the water you're drinking."

Lord Abewell swallowed hard and quickly placed the glass back on a table with a shaking hand.

"That was an order, not a suggestion," scolded the king. "Tomorrow, you understand?" Drago stomped off to the door.

"Tomorrow?" asked Lord Abewell with a low voice. He was unsure of his task the next day, but he added, "Yes, Your Majesty." The councilor approached the door.

King Drago opened the door showing the way out to the councilor. "Ask General Althar to come to my office," said the king, giving Lord Abewell a dark look.

"Immediately," responded the councilor, reaching the hallway hesitatingly. The councilor stopped in midstride, but then continued to find General Althar.

King Drago slammed the door and waited impatiently for the high rank general.

I need strict supervision and control of the entire process, thought Drago while playing with a pen once again. He wanted to gain the admiration and trust of his entire kingdom. He thought controlling the food distribution was the fastest and best solution to achieve his ambitious goal.

It did not take long for General Althar to knock on the Diamond Office's door.

"General Althar?" asked the king, stretching his neck.

"At your service!" responded the general with a ringing voice.

"Come in," ordered King Drago. "I'm taking over our food supply. As of tomorrow, the Market will be our new distribution center," said King Drago without giving a chance to

General Althar to complete his military salute.

"How can I help?" asked the general. He already knew that King Drago was eager to change the lives of the Brightalians.

"Finally, someone smart around here!" King Drago's pen dropped to the floor. "Early in the morning, go with a regiment, a large one to intimidate the merchants, and confiscate every single stand," King Drago explained coldly. His eyes shone.

"Consider it done!" General Althar picked up the pen and handed it to King Drago. Althar liked the new king. Drago was aggressive and quick in making decisions, an opposite to King Alessio who was too cautious and prudent.

"Good answer," said King Drago, smiling broadly. "We will then prepare a—" The king thought for a minute or two. "Let's call it the *Dragon-box*, a basic food basket for each family," said King Drago. "I love my inspiration!" The king prided himself with a mock laugh.

"Our people will thank you," expressed General Althar, supporting the king's initiative.

"Ah! One more thing," added King Drago, pushing his chair forward until his black robe hit the edge of the desk.

"Listening," said the general, leaning toward the royal desk. He did not know what to expect. Any outrageous idea could come out of the king's mind. But he was ready to execute every command.

"If Lord Abewell gets in your way, send him home," advised the king with a gruff voice.

"Home will be his next stop." General Althar stood with a fixed face and giving a military salute, he added, "If Your Majesty allows me, I must go now. Tomorrow will be a busy day."

"Go ahead." King Drago shook his head. "Remember, I'm counting on you and your people."

King Drago rested his crossed legs on top of the desk, and

with both hands behind his head, he let out a malevolent laugh. "Power, power. It's all mine."

Definitely, change got to Brightalia. Way too soon! The well-advertised Dragon-box was not what people received. The basic basket was not enough for any given family. Nobody was thankful as General Althar predicted.

The food problem never improved. How would the people survive? How would parents feed their children? Villagers were desperate to satisfy their hunger. The kingdom was about to collapse.

The real Dragon-box stayed at Diamond Palace where there was an overabundance of food that could feed the entire village. King Drago was having fun. He threw parties every night. Only his friends were living a happy life. Whole baskets of fruit, vegetables, bread, and even meat got thrown out at the end of every day. The slop pails of the palace were rich with food for the pigs.

One afternoon, Martina decided to give away all the leftover food, even if it was almost rotten. In a matter of minutes, there was a huge line at the east side gate of Diamond Palace. Mercy helped the princess distribute the brown bags.

The information quickly filtered to the ears of Drago by one of the security guards. The king did not hesitate to clomp outside and check for himself.

"What do you think you're doing?" Drago fired off the question with a shout. He rushed to Martina and snatched away the bag of food that the princess was about to hand to the next person in line.

Martina jumped in place. She was going to response when Mercy intervened.

"Your Majesty, my family as well as many people at Enna Valley are dying. They do not have anything to eat," the nanny respectfully said.

"I asked Mercy to help me. We can't keep wasting food when we have so many hungry people," Martina added. "Don't you see this line?"

Enzo, who was twentieth in line, added from the back, "My mom is very sick. Please let us have this food."

"You said you're going to help us, King Drago!" added another villager. "We're hungry!"

"Of course! Take it all." King Drago had no choice but to support his sister's initiative. "More servants will be on the way to help," the king finished with a forced smile. Then he roughly grabbed Martina by the arm and hustled her inside.

"Let go of my arm. You're hurting me!" Martina tripped over a step and almost fell.

"I'm really going to hurt you if you continue getting in my way!" barked Drago.

"I wish we can work together."

"Never Martina, never!"

Some servants who were passing by stared at the king.

"What are you looking at?" Drago yelled. "Go outside and help with the dirty bags."

The maidservants rushed out in fear.

"Drago! Is that really you?" Martina was starting to believe that Drago had lost his mind. "I don't recognize you anymore."

"Don't waste my time, sis. Get out of my sight if you want to stay in this palace!" said Drago, making an effort to lower his voice.

It was obvious that King Drago was not seeing the overspending at the palace, and he did not care about the needs of the kingdom. There was only one person who did, Martina. But Drago did not allow her to help. Who was going to save Brightalia now? Hope looked farther away each day.

CHAPTER FIFTEEN

The next morning, Martina's eyes flew open very early. The first thing she noticed was that her diary was not black anymore. It had completely turned orange, and the word on its cover was "create". Martina pondered the word for a moment or two. Then, she was ready to leave Diamond Palace.

The princess dashed out of the room and crept downstairs. On her way out to the passage that led to the stables, she bumped into Mercy.

The nanny was carrying a basket with freshly laundered clothes. "Where is the princess going in such a rush?" asked Mercy.

"I'm going to the beach. Please don't tell anybody," whispered Martina, making sure that no one else would listen.

"By yourself? Be careful out there!" Mercy said in a protective tone.

"Don't worry, Mercy. I'll be back tonight. I promise," added Martina. She knew she could trust Mercy.

"Take care, my little princess," insisted Mercy.

"I'm not little anymore!" shouted Martina, hurrying back to the stable.

The nanny mounted the stairs to Martina's room. She placed the basket on the ottoman inside the dressing room and began her cleaning routine. It was so effortless. She pulled out an ivory wand from under her apron, waved it around and began to chant. All the clothes flew to the right place. She noticed some sand in a few corners of the room, and with another move of her wand, the bedroom floor was spotless. She even added a new tank for Tattoo, the betta fish. In a couple of minutes, the suite was impeccable and neat for when the princess would come back.

At the beach, the sun was dazzling over the sea horizon. The peaceful sand island made Martina feel right at home. The soft breeze lifted Martina's curls into the air. What a welcoming sensation! She sat down and touched the crystal sand. She observed the endless amount of sand.

That day, Martina decided it was time to use her magical powers. Her kingdom was falling, and she was determined to help her people regardless of her brother's opposition. She pulled out Drago's old drawing, the one she had taken from his room one night. She stared at the paper.

Martina closed her eyes and imagined the unique house with a fresh beach look. It was not a shock that the house that she pictured in her mind was right in front of her.

What happened next was the total surprise.

Martina's eyes started glittering. Their violet color greatly intensified. Warm bright violet rays came out of her eyes and wrapped around the beach house like a tornado.

The princess fell down to the sand. She felt weak, but her emotion was stronger than her tiredness. She climbed back to her feet, still lost as to what had just happened. She walked close to the house and felt how it was solid as a rock. The light soft sand was compressed together into her most wonderful creation.

Martina was breathless with excitement. "I did it! My dream came true!" Her natural powers had shown. Her violet eyes had the magic to make her sand figures permanent.

Martina had built a house on the sand island! Something that her parents had thought was impossible. There was nobody to celebrate with, but she was sure it was a magical day, one that was going to change her life and those of many others.

Martina was not ready to stop. The following day she went back again to Amo Island. It was very windy, and dense clouds covered the blue sky. The sunlight was barely visible. It was an unusual day in the sunny kingdom. But it was still a perfect day for the princess.

The fresh beach house now enhanced the stunning view of Amo Island; exactly how she left it the night before. The design was very simple, free of clutter. Inspired by the building in Drago's drawing, it was very modern and completely different from the Brightalia architecture.

Martina needed to test the limits of her magical powers despite her mother's advice. She wanted to try something different and go beyond her comfort zone. She needed to push her magical powers further, to their fullest potential. *Can I build a permanent structure on the water?* A pier became Martina's next desirable task.

Looking at the agitated sea waves, Martina sat on the sand. She immediately closed her eyes and imagined a long pier decorated with comfortable benches all along the walkway.

Soon she felt the warm sensation. The bright violet rays from her eyes were so intense that the pier became a solid structure as it appeared from under the sea. The clouds also became a purple color. It seemed as if a big explosion covered the island. Crystal water dripped down the sand formation until the most impressive pier fully emerged and became totally visible.

Martina ran to the pier. She touched every single pillar and every stone bench. She sat at the end of the pier, closed her eyes, and let the sound of the splashing water delight her ears. *What a wonderful and peaceful experience! How could this be dangerous?* Small drops started coming down from the sky. A light rain approached the sand island.

Martina stayed to watch the sunset. Soon after that, she left what had become her second home.

The clouds had darkened, and the ride home was somewhat rough with the heavy rain. Soaked in water, Martina hopped off White Diamond at the stables. At once, she went inside and charged up the palace stairs. But right across from the corridor was Drago. He was walking away from the princess. Martina stopped short after she saw him. But the king had already heard the agitated steps and turned back.

King Drago walked toward Martina. His eyebrows arched.

Sensing Drago's presence made Martina flinch. She remained silent.

The king observed a creamy wall that he could not recall seeing before. "Who painted this space?" He stood there for a short moment. Then he pulled back and moved away from the wall, murmuring, "It doesn't look bad at all."

Martina sighed, feeling relief. She was behind the new sand wall that had just allowed her to hide from her brother. The princess had found a way to make herself invisible. She smiled, touched the magical wall, and headed to her suite.

Martina had a challenging task ahead of her. She wanted to build an entire sand village with farming instruments for her people. Easing the food crisis became her goal.

The princess started going to Amo Island during the night to avoid conflicts with her brother. After everybody went to sleep, Martina sneaked out of the dark palace. She hid under a purple cloak. On her mare, White Diamond, she galloped over the mountain road, crossing the long bridge that led to the island. Her project was going very well until one particular night.

Leaning against the stairway railing, Drago looked down as Martina escaped to the beach.

The princess did not see him.

"Martina! Martina!" his teeth sparkled with his broad smile. Drago was already suspicious about Martina having powers and, even worse, about her going to Amo Island. "If it is you, you'll have fun tonight!" He exploded into a loud guffaw that made the walls of the palace tremble.

At the beach, Martina had built most of the tall and narrow houses. Each residence had a long field in the back with farming tools. The sand village was pretty much complete. The night was warm, and she still had some extra time. The princess decided to add a plaza. She sat on the sand next to a house. Strangely, she heard something, like a growl. She turned her head and saw nothing.

White Diamond snorted and lifted her forelegs up in the air.

"Whoa! Take it easy, buddy. What's wrong?" Martina tapped her mare on her flank. She moved to the side of the house standing against the wall. She turned her head slowly. Her heart dropped to a speed of zero when she spotted a pair of yellow eyes. They were those of a ralthor, a wild predator that resembled a cross between a wolf and a panther. She stuck to the wall and quietly began to scuffle to the entrance of the house. But strong paws reached her back, clubbing her down with a sudden swipe. More eyes appeared from behind, barking at the princess. Martina rolled over and caught a glance of the hungry wet mouths full of sharp teeth, all in front of her. A pack of five angry ralthors yapped, ready to attack Martina. She scrambled to her feet and stumbled to the door. But she could not make it to safety. One of the wild beasts caught up with her. Its powerful paws dragged her down to the sand again. The ferocious animal pawed at her chest. The rest of the ralthors approached. She kicked one of them with her bare foot.

"Where is the white eagle when I need it?" wailed Martina, as she extended one of her arms in a desperate search of a stick or anything hard. But all she could grab was a handful of sand. She tossed it at the greedy animal. The beast moved to the side, shaking its head.

Without giving the princess a break, another voracious animal launched its fury over her. It ripped her dress with its razor claws, leaving three deep scratches on her chest. She tried to crawl backward to get away from the vicious ralthors. Her attempt was fruitless. She raised her left hand to parry the interminable attack. She then maneuvered with her other hand to defend herself. She pounded the beast's face with her fist. But she ended up more disoriented than the animal from the soreness of her knuckles. The scary ralthors had completely surrounded their tasty prey. Martina felt helpless. She was getting weaker by the second. Sharp fangs clamped onto her left shin. Her leg burned with fresh cuts. She tried her magic, but she had no strength.

"Help, please!" yelped Martina as if somebody could hear her. At that point, everything seemed to switch to slow motion.

Martina's vision blurred. She was in agonizing pain. Her legs went numb.

All of a sudden, soft steps in old leather sandals came close to Martina's head. A staff tip sank into the soft sand. She did not notice. She just sensed the heavy breathing of the blue ralthors as their jaws penetrated her skin. The old man, standing behind Martina, raised his silver staff and chanted a magic curse. *Crashing Vento Hexan!* A powerful stream of hot air shot from the long stick onto the wild animals, sending them soaring high in the air. Martina tried to lift her head. The old guy then waggled his staff, and the animals crashed to the sand with a severe blow. The frightened beasts disappeared, howling and crying. The old man also popped to nothing like a soap bubble.

Martina gasped, trying to find some air. She struggled to sit. Her body refused to move. She was not sure who had helped her. She just knew she was safe now. She stayed still staring at the moon. It was a full moon night. She coughed and felt chills running down her body. Her eyes closed without her realizing it.

Around midnight, the princess woke up. She was confused. She did not know if she had dreamed about the ralthors' dreadful incident. She made her strongest effort to recover her wits. It was her aching body that gave her the easy answer. Her legs and arms were also sore and swollen. Her mouth was dry asking for water. She tore one of her sleeves and covered the wound on her leg with the piece of cloth. She stood and limped to a house warily.

Martina waited a while and continued with her ambitious goal, the Sand Plaza. The princess closed her eyes and let the structure form in her imagination. The plaza sat at the center of the village facing the pier. At its back, there was a small church and an open space for a future market. All the houses wrapped around the plaza making a "U" shape. Martina wanted every house to enjoy the ocean view and her marvelous pier. A large fountain was the main attraction of the Sand Plaza. Its water was clear during the day, but at night a spray of sand crystals unfolded a picturesque array of colors.

Battling adverse weather or weird animals, Martina kept spending her nights at the beach until her dream was complete, becoming a tangible reality. Amo Island had turned into a new city with everything people needed. It even had a Bladeking field. It was not very large, yet it had a unique twist. Martina added obstacles serving as fighting barriers and hiding blocks to make the game more interesting.

Rumors gradually spread about the new sand place. Day after day, the creamy village started turning into the green color of new crops. Farmers did not know who to thank for such a great gift, but they all hoped that one day they would find out who was the generous creator of such a magnificent place.

CHAPTER SIXTEEN

At a long distance, Martina could not be any happier about Amo Island. Every time she heard a new family had moved to the sand village, it was a big pump of love to her heart. But at a short distance, the princess was bereaved. She observed how Drago continued his ambitious climb to the top of his own ladder. She spied on him through tiny peepholes on the doors, made of her magical sand. She stayed out of sight as much as possible. Every new announcement was worse than the previous one. She was bemused by all the nonsense reforms imposed by her brother. She did not know how to stop his madness, but she knew she was not giving up in her desire to help.

One morning, Martina decided to visit the Market. There was a regiment of soldiers at the entrance and a long line of peasants turning in their products. The princess went inside and looked around. Most of the stands had been confiscated. Only a few survived. She got to the end of the mart and saw the quaint table full of clear containers with water. She was glad it was still there.

"Ufff! Couldn't you find a cart closer to the entrance?" said

Martina, trying to get Enzo's attention. He was fixing a net.

"Princess Martina! I'm surprised to see you here!" said Enzo, blowing the hair off his forehead. "This place is in ruins!"

"Well, it's still okay!" Martina had not lost her hope that things would improve. Enzo was right. More than half of the stalls were indeed empty. And who was cleaning the Market? It seemed like that job had been eliminated. But Martina was there for another reason. "I need to go to Lusha Land. I must understand the situation there."

"What? Are you nuts?" Enzo dropped his net and turned his stupefied gaze to Martina. "That place can look like a battlefield some days. It's not safe to go there."

"And I want you to go with me," quickly followed up Martina.

"Even worse! Volunteer suicide," Enzo grumbled. He tossed the tangled net into an empty box. "I quit my job there after a loose arrow almost hit me. My mother said I might not be so lucky the second time. Border fights between Brightalia and Castella are more common every day. They happen without notice. Anybody can be caught in the middle of one."

Martina moved closer to the stand. "Precisely! You know the area."

"I'm not going."

"Do you trust me?"

"Hmm!" Enzo thought for a moment. "Well, yes!"

"Okay, we're going." Martina picked up some of the empty containers as if she were going to help Enzo put away everything and clean up the cart.

"What are you doing?" Enzo took the containers away from Martina's hands. "I said I'm not going."

"You said yes!" Martina crossed her arms and frowned, pretending to be mad.

"It was a different question!"

"Then I'm going by myself." The princess started walking away from the cart.

"You'll get lost in less than a second."

Martina stopped in mid-step and turned around. "Then come with me."

Enzo heaved a long sigh and with some hesitation, he agreed, "Okay, I'll go with you." He did not look too convinced. "But only to the beginning of Lusha, right after the stream that runs behind my house."

"Great!" Martina smiled with excitement. She grabbed some containers again.

"Not that quick, Princess," Enzo responded, looking at his tank. "I must sell all my fish before we leave."

"Oh! I see." Martina moved to the back of the stand.

"What is it with you now?"

"I'm helping." The princess raised two containers. "Buy one fish and get the second one half price!" She waved the container around.

"Martina!" said Enzo with an astonished look. "A princess selling my fish?"

"Buy two fish and get the third one *free!*" chanted Martina as a villager came to the cart. Shortly after that, she heard a familiar voice.

"You! Here?" It was King Drago who stopped in front of the table. Eight guards stood behind him. "And with Fish-face?" He was outraged to find his sister there.

"Drago!" affirmed Martina. Her face would have looked better if she had seen a ghost. Her heartbeat elevated.

"Go home!" ordered Drago right away. He signaled one of the guards to approach the princess.

Martina did not move from where she was.

"She's doing nothing wrong. She's just helping." Enzo stepped in to defend Martina.

Drago ignored him. He saw that the guard stood beside the princess ready to escort her out of the place. "Let me rephrase that … you're leaving … *now!*" he yelled at his sister.

"I'm going nowhere with you!" quickly reacted the princess. This time, Martina was not willing to follow her brother's orders.

There was an instant tense silence. Enzo and even the guards showed shocked faces.

Drago pounded his fist on the cart in disgust. His face flushed red. He did not expect his sister to confront him. He pointed a finger at Martina and added in a threatening tone. "Fine! You'll have to return to Diamond Palace sooner or later." Then he turned his back on the princess and walked away followed by the line of guards.

Martina tried to calm herself down. She sighed and reached for the next container. "Eating fish is healthy. The third one is *free!*"

Time flew, and in less than two hours the table was empty. Enzo put his tank away and turned to Martina. "Thank you! I'd have never guessed a royal person … a real princess would sell stinky fish at a village marketplace."

"Oh! That was nothing," responded the princess walking toward the back doors of the market. There was the small coach.

"*Woohoo!* Am I going in a royal carriage?" said Enzo with a thrill, exiting the market.

"Of course, King of the Sea!" smiled Martina as she scooted over making room for Enzo to sit alongside her.

"Let me show my best royal posture," said Enzo, looking like a statue.

Martina just stared at him. Enzo was so genuine, simple and content compared to her brother. She wished Drago would be at least a little bit like him, less grouchy.

Shortly, the royal carriage left the market and took a narrow dirt road that led to a green meadow. There, they decided to enjoy the grass. Martina and Enzo talked as though they had known each other for a long time. It was a breezy afternoon. The grass rippled under their feet.

Enzo noticed a scar on Martina's leg. It was from the ralthors' bites. "What happened to you?"

Martina looked down. "Oh, that's nothing, a stupid branch from a famous oak tree at home."

"Famous! That reminds me." Enzo scratched the fish on his cheek. "Do you want to hear a fish joke?" asked the market seller.

"How can I miss it?" grinned Martina cheerfully.

"Here I go! What do you call a betta fish without an eye?" asked Enzo.

"Um! I have no idea," said Martina frowning.

"A betta fsssh ..." answered Enzo.

They both guffawed as they crossed a small rock bridge. Enzo surely made Martina's time enjoyable.

"This is the beginning of the stream that runs at the back of my house," said Enzo, pointing at the narrow river.

As they got closer to the mountains, small houses became visible. Then, they made a turn to a long peculiar road. At the end of the street, a modest yellow cottage stood out. It had three steps that led to a wooden white porch. On a corner were a hanging pot of white flowers and an old rocking chair.

"Welcome home!" said Enzo as he opened a creaking fence.

The creek ran along the back of the cottage, surrounded by vivid green areas. The banks of the stream had pines and old big trees. Butterflies and blue jays glazed the top leaves of the trees.

"Wow, I love the nature, the stream, the birds!" said Martina with delight.

"I'm glad you enjoy my deep sea," teased Enzo.

Enzo started telling Martina the real story about his fish. He explained how each morning he went to the stream to catch the fish to then sell them at the Market.

"You must be an expert by now."

"I do my best," said Enzo, glancing at a troop of bettas swimming by.

After carefully listening to Enzo's story, Martina asked, "Is that Lusha Land?" She pointed to the other side of the stream.

"Yes!" assured Enzo. "Crossing the stream is the fastest way to get there, but you'll have to get your feet wet."

But Martina was already in the water. "Too easy!" That was only until she slipped and fell down with a splash.

Enzo, who waded closely behind Martina, was caught by surprise. He swayed on his feet and landed next to the princess. "Are you hurt?" he asked with concern.

"No, I'm okay!" the princess said blushing.

Their faces came close to a kiss. "I thought all royal people were stuck-up. But ... but ... you're different."

Martina's pink cheeks became like red flames of fire. "I'm just a regular person living in a palace."

Enzo offered Martina a hand to help her up and finish crossing the stream.

"Finally, Lusha Land!" Martina shook the water off her dress.

"Yup!" confirmed Enzo, twisting his wet shirt. He walked into the big extension of land. There was some visible smoke to the north. Enzo decided to borrow a couple of horses to show Martina the area.

"Brightalia has been battling for years to recover its part of Lusha territory." Martina observed the harvest area. It was not very extensive. "I don't see too many fields," she went on. Her horse picked up its own natural canter.

"When the conflicts with Castella began, everything started going downhill. The Castellian soldiers have no mercy, just like their king." Enzo rode to a street. "Do you see the big gates across the road?" He pointed at some brown doors.

"Impressive!" said the princess, turning toward the gates. Her horse slowed to a walk.

"That's the entrance to one of the few ranches that remains in the area. It is well-known for its coffee plantation," pointed out Enzo.

Martina inhaled deeply. "Yes! Fresh ground coffee." She saw a few workers plowing the plains.

"It's the best coffee in town. Mr. Acardi is the owner," said Enzo.

"My dad couldn't survive a morning without a cup of coffee," commented Martina, staring at the peasants. "What about the one across?"

"A cornfield."

As they trotted their horses along the plantations, Enzo described each of them. Martina was correct. He knew the area pretty well. They made it to the free lands, deep into the woods. They passed fallen logs and trees. Then, they let the horses rest and drink some water.

Martina could sense the smell of burning grass. Dry leaves swiveled around her feet.

Suddenly, Enzo heard a weird noise. He stretched his neck and looked into the trees.

"What is it?" asked Martina. One of the horses raised his head up high and snorted.

"Shhh!" Enzo kept eyeing some oak trees. He moved back a few steps, near a big dead trunk.

Martina hurried next to Enzo. Her eyes widened, trying to spot something, anything. But what she saw was the horses racing away from them. "Wait," she screamed at the stallions.

"Don't wait, run! Run fast!" Enzo said to Martina with a frightened look on his face. "We're under attack."

Martina quickly sprinted through the maze of trees, right behind Enzo. She did not look back, but she just imagined crossbows ready to be shot at them.

"Look out!" warned Enzo.

They jumped over a group of logs and landed on a dense patch of leaves. Their steps grew muffled by the extensive blanket of bracken fronds that covered the forest floor.

It was then when Martina saw three raging ralthors catching up to her. The nasty breathing of the predatory beasts got closer by the second.

"This way!" Enzo shouted.

They continued to run until they reached the top of a steep hill.

Martina stumbled and ended up rolling all the way down. Her mind did not have time to realize that it was going to hurt and burn too. Dry branches and skinny sticks scratched her face and arms.

"Martina!" Enzo called out. He also struggled his way down to the low ground. He made it after flipping over a couple of times. "Are you okay?"

Martina gasped trying to get some air to her lungs. "That's what I call a rough landing," she slowly said, sitting up just a foot away from Enzo.

Dust covered their bodies. They were spent.

There was a short moment of quietness. But the vicious ralthors were not giving up. The three beasts made it there too, right in front of Martina and Enzo.

Enzo quickly got up, and with a single impulse, he lifted Martina to get her to safety.

The princess climbed onto a tree faster than a monkey. She extended her arm down, but it was too late. "Enzo," cried out Martina.

The three hungry animals had already surrounded Enzo. He was trapped between the ralthors and the tree. The peasant was an instant away from facing his death. In no time, the ralthors' sharp teeth would clamp around his sweaty neck.

Against all her fears, Martina did not hesitate to expose her secret. Just as the first ralthor lunged itself at Enzo, Martina gathered her magic. She waved an arm and sent a sand sword that hit the feral animal right in its chest.

The wounded beast fell backward with a loud howl. Limping and crying, the scary ralthor went away. But the two other predators were already on top of Enzo.

Enzo maneuvered to push them away. He was covered in blue fur. Four yellow eyes looked at him with fury. "Get away from me," wailed Enzo. He was a perfect fish on a hook. He had no way to escape.

Martina saw the terror on Enzo's face, as one of the beasts was about to lock his jaw around the tasty prey. The princess summoned again her magical powers. This time, a handful of sand spears hit both animals right before their deadly teeth wrapped around the poor villager. Then, she covered them with a giant spider web just to double anchor them in place.

Enzo ended up completely baffled on the ground as he watched how the growling ralthors were left lying beside him, well trapped. Soon, his expression transformed from perplexed to doubtful. "So, you're a witch!"

"Excuse me?" Martina was offended. She had just saved Enzo's life.

Enzo's hand flew to his mouth. "No, no," he tried to correct his comment. "I mean you're a good sorceress!"

"What?" The princess jumped down from the tree, landing in a crouch.

Enzo realized his words still did not sound quite nice and blurted out an explanation. "What I'm really trying to say is that you're a princess with power. I'd never imagined—"

"Shh," interrupted Martina softly putting a finger on Enzo's lips. "It was the least I could do."

"Thank you!" said Enzo, inclining his head.

Suddenly, the scene shocked Martina. Her eyebrows rose up. She remembered the prophecy the old man gave her years ago at the beach. "I've just saved a special boy. Now I can save my kingdom!" She held a steady gaze at Enzo's left cheek. "The fish on your face."

"Yeeeaah," Enzo answered slowly. He looked puzzled.

"It makes you special."

"Sure, special," Enzo agreed, not to disagree. "You know! My mom tells me that too. She thinks I'm a special boy," he added, with a light giggle. Enzo did not believe the birthmark on his cheek made him any different from the rest of the people. To him, it was the same as somebody having a tattoo.

"Special and lucky," Martina added with a wink.

"That's for sure! My mom was wrong." Enzo knew this was a fact, and he could prove it. "I was lucky—"

"A second time!" they both said together, like a small choir. Martina and Enzo looked at each other and roared with laughter.

Martina had used her power to save Enzo, letting her secret out. She also told Enzo about the sand village. She explained how she had secretly experimented with her magical powers over the years. Then she went on and also thanked Enzo for sharing his dad's message with her. The phase: *Whenever you dream, dream big* was a key inspiration to start using her powers to create a new town. She invited Enzo to visit the new Amo Island.

Enzo listened with great attention. He was impressed with Martina's story, one that was actually real.

Back where the small carriage was, Enzo thanked Martina one more time. "I owe you my life," expressed Enzo with a deep bow and a kiss to the palm of the princess.

"Good-bye, King of the Sea," added Martina, curtsying.

Enzo could not resist and gave Martina a tight hug.

The princess smiled without making any resistance.

"Sorry!" added Enzo with embarrassment. He let go of Martina's waist.

"That's okay," Martina said. A warm blush deepened in her face from nose to ears.

One last smile at each other, and Martina and Enzo started the separate ways back to their homes.

Princess Martina really enjoyed spending time with Enzo. It was nice having someone to share her life experiences, jokes, and even adventures. Her thoughts rapidly took her to Jupiter. She wondered if the kind peasant liked her. *He seems to care about me. He is quite handsome. He makes me laugh. I don't feel lonely anymore.* Martina fantasized about spending another day with Enzo until she finally made it to Diamond Palace.

A half-moon brightened Martina's room. Its natural light gave color to her magical wooden box. But it also gave a distinct shade of pink to the old diary. Yes, the diary had changed color again! The entire book was pink and the word on the cover was "friendship".

"Enzo!" she smiled. Martina read her journal, but to her surprise, a drawing appeared on the last page. It was the first time that the diary showed her an illustration.

What is this sketch? wondered Martina. She observed

carefully. The princess did not know she was about to make a weird discovery.

CHAPTER SEVENTEEN

The drawing showed a cat. But the curious fact was that it had five legs, and it was in Drago's room. It was late. Still, Martina did not think about it twice. She headed to his room. She pushed the door slightly ajar and popped her head into the bedroom. It was empty. Drago was not there.

A furry tail stuck out of Drago's bed. Martina was startled when she saw it. The diary was correct. She carefully approached the animal to take a closer look. *Yes, indeed! A cat,* she confirmed. What was a cat doing there? Strange but still possible. Martina just imagined a new pet to play with. Maybe that was the reason the journal was showing it to her.

"Come out, cutie!" called Martina. But there was no response. The cat, or even worse the tail, did not move. The princess went ahead and pulled the blue cat by the tail to get it out from under the bed.

"Aaaah!" Martina screamed her lungs out in fear. Her eyes were as big as two baseballs. There was no cat, just a tail. In less than a second, the princess dropped the tail back to the floor. She was horrified and scared. She felt as if her heart had stopped beating. That was the end of her nice pet story.

What was Drago doing? Did it have anything to do with the red book? But the scene did not get any better. When Martina glanced at Drago's desk, it was then she felt dizzy and almost about to throw up. The cat bones were right in front of her. Hands pressed to her mouth in panic, Martina managed to move a few steps closer to the table. The stinky smell only worsened her nausea. She quickly covered her nose.

A paper lay flat on the side of the desk. Written in faded black ink, it was a spell that explained that dark powers could be gained if a sacrifice of a five-legged blue animal was made.

Drago was acquiring dark powers. Martina wished she could deny it. She refused to believe her brother had learned black magic. But the evidence was very clear. King Drago was turning to the dark side of magic.

Martina rushed out of the room. She did not know who to look for or what to do. She entered the library room. She needed some time to pull herself together. The discovery was hard to bear. What was next?

No chance to think about an answer.

"Ah, you're back!" King Drago entered the library through the opposite door.

Martina jumped. "Drago!" She could see the devious grin plastered on her brother's face. She moved away from him. "What are you doing?"

"No! The question here is what are *you* doing? King Drago walked closer to his sister, his boots clopping against the floor.

"What do you mean?"

"I knew you had magical power, but did you build the sand village? Tell me now!" demanded Drago, holding up an accusing finger, one that almost touched the princess's nose.

Martina was not sure what lay ahead, but she went for the truth. "Yes, it was me," she answered with a broken voice. She moved backward a few steps.

"You can try all you want, but you'll never take the throne away from me!" scolded Drago. He was fuming.

"No, you're wrong!" Martina fumbled to explain. It was never her intention. "I was just trying to help."

"Leave Diamond Palace, Martina," Drago ordered. The king strode across the room and stopped at a window turning his eyes away from his sister.

"No, please!" Martina cried. "I'll never do that to you. I don't want to be a queen."

"I tried to warn you with the ralthors' attacks," snarled Drago, looking outside.

"It was you?" Martina gasped in shock. She was totally dumbstruck.

"But you did not stop." Drago turned back.

Martina gave Drago an astonished look. "You're becoming a monster."

"Enough!" Drago's scream echoed in the room. The prince got closer, and his penetrating eyes looked directly at Martina. "It's my time to shine, and you won't ruin my plan. Leave now, Martina!" barked Drago, pounding his fist on a table.

Disbelief spread across Martina's face. Drago had lost his mind completely. But still, he was all she had. He was her family. "Please! I promise, I won't get in your way!" she begged.

Drago was furious and did not feel any compassion for his sister. He feared Martina's powers. He just wanted her out of his way, out of his sight. He did not want to injure his sister, but he was out of control.

"I said leave my palace right now!" yelled Drago as he started throwing porcelain figurines at Martina.

"Please! Stop!" Martina pleaded.

Whimpering and shaking, Martina tottered around

in the room trying to get away from the flying pieces of broken porcelain.

"Please, Drago! Don't hurt me," Martina yelped.

A rush of anger arose inside Drago. Harder and faster he was shattering everything in the room. There was a loud bang, as Drago hurled a huge display cabinet against the floor. Pieces of glass crashed across the room.

Drago's face flushed red. He swept his arm across a credenza and sent Murano glass statuettes crashing to the floor.

Martina struggled to get to the door. Suddenly, her shoe got entangled in a rug. The princess tripped over a table and fell to the floor.

Drago could not control his anger. With insane power, he threw more figurines at his sister. He smashed a large flower vase against the wall, just above the princess.

Martina projected her violet rays at her brother. But at the same time, Drago extended his arm. A strong red beam of light shot against Martina's rays. In no time, the red light overpowered Martina's magic and aimed straight at the vase pieces.

Martina shielded her face, but a shard of glass cut her nose, and multiple tiny pieces fell into her eyes. Martina doubled over in pain. She felt as if a sharp needle had pricked her eyes. She tried to open them, but she could see nothing.

"My eyes," wept Martina. Her pain tripled knowing that her eyes were the heart of her magical powers.

Giorgina heard the booming noises in the library room and ran downstairs looking for Mercy. "Prince Drago is hurting Martina. He's going to kill her," said Giorgina with a trembling voice.

The nanny rushed up the stairway. "Martina, Martina!" Mercy screamed desperately. She stopped at the door. Her eyes widened and her heart lurched at the dreadful scene. It seemed as though a bomb had been detonated inside the room.

Mercy could see that she was too late.

Martina was slumped on the rug. She did not move. Her head faced the floor. Pieces of glass covered her body.

"My princess! Can you hear me?" cried Mercy, running to rescue her beloved little girl.

Martina turned over with the gentle help of Mercy. The deep wound on Martina's nose frightened Mercy. The nanny quickly removed her apron and cleaned Martina's face.

Martina sat in pain. She squinted, but her vision was blurry. "I'm okay," said the princess, pressing the apron to her nose.

"What are you waiting for? Leave my palace!" barked Drago. He kicked a table and flipped it upside down.

Mercy kneeled down and grabbed Drago's hand. "Please, stop hurting your sister," begged Mercy.

Drago breathed deeply and plopped down onto a sofa.

"My princess, go! Go, Martina!" said Mercy with a broken heart.

Martina got up, but after two weak steps, dizziness returned her to the floor. She heaved a great sigh and crawled to the door with difficulty. The princess firmly held the doorframe to stand. A minute went by, and she could only wince. Giorgina and two other servants in the corridor rushed to help Martina and carried her to her bedroom.

"Thank you! Leave me in my dressing room," requested Martina.

Mercy rushed inside the room, but Martina did not give her a chance to say a word.

"Mercy, get White Diamond ready. I must leave now!" implored Martina.

Mercy immediately followed Martina's orders even though she wished Martina would never leave Diamond Palace.

Stumbling around her room, Martina grabbed her wooden box and her diary. She put them in a cinch sack. The princess heaved the drawstring backpack onto her shoulder, and tripping on everything in her way, Martina went downstairs looking for her nanny. Her vision had not cleared.

"Mercy! Mercy!" Martina called.

"I'm here, my princess. White Diamond is waiting for you," said Mercy with a profound pain in her heart. The little girl she had seen grow up was about to leave in deep pain. Mercy grabbed Martina by the hand and ushered her to the passage that led straight toward the stables.

Martina touched the animal and said, "You are a well-trained mare, the best at avoiding obstacles. We can do this. I trust you, White Diamond."

White Diamond nodded at Martina.

Mercy grabbed Martina's violet cloak and giving it to her, she said, "Take good care of yourself. I hope to see you soon."

"I'll be on Amo Island," responded the princess, throwing her cloak on.

Martina pulled the hood up, and right away, she was on her way out of her only home, Diamond Palace. The princess made a quick stop at Piano Plaza. She tugged White Diamond's reins, and the docile mare slowed to a stop. Martina slipped out of the saddle and slumped to the ground. At the bottom of her dad's statue, Martina let her tears out.

"I miss you so much, Father," Martina cried. "I know you'll always be in my heart, but it's not easy. I'm losing my strength." There at the plaza, a memory from her first trip to the beach surfaced. Martina remembered she assured her dad to use her powers to serve her kingdom. She needed to continue her mission. As fragile as she felt, Martina wiped her tears, caught her breath, and climbed her mare again.

White Diamond started her slow gallop to the sand island. The ride was a little bit longer than usual, but White Diamond did not disappoint the princess. Her heart pumped with joy when she heard the unmistakable sound of the seawater running below her. They were crossing the long bridge to the beach and made it to the pier.

There, Martina climbed down from White Diamond and sat on the last bench facing the water. "What are we going to do now?" She knew her magical eyes were her most precious and valuable means to help others. The princess pulled her diary out of her cinch sack. She tried to feel the letters, but the pages were smooth as silk.

White Diamond lay down at the feet of the princess. Martina gently touched her mane. "Some people are blind because they can't see. Others are blind because they don't want to see. I hope Drago and I will see tomorrow!" She sat still for a couple of hours. She listened to the birds passing by and to someone paddling what she guessed was a small canoe. She even detected the running legs of a crab on the pier.

The wind picked up quite a bit, and Martina felt the cool breeze of the night. Some chills got to her bones. She curled up on the bench and rested her head on the diary. She recalled the homeless man she ran into one day at Piano Plaza. She wished she had someone to cover her with a blanket. Nobody came to her rescue.

Darkness surrounded the princess completely. Even the moon was hidden behind dense clouds. Martina counted the rippling waves trying to distract her mind from the unpleasant feeling of coldness. But it was tiredness that finally let the princess fall into a dreamless sleep.

The next morning, Martina woke up quite disoriented. It was not until she touched her swollen nose that all the memories from the previous day came back. The good news, her vision had partially cleared. She sat up and all her body ached, especially her neck. The diary was not a comfortable pillow at all. Far worse was the emptiness in her stomach. It growled louder than a lion. Martina realized she had not eaten in a day. She dug to the bottom of the sack, but all she had was her wooden box.

"I'm starving!" groaned Martina, making an effort to stand up. She was very weak and her legs did not cooperate very much. She decided to head to the sand village sure that somebody would offer something to eat. She held on tight to White Diamond's reins. She made it to the small market and then, as any new commoner getting to the village, the princess searched for an empty house. She carried her drawstring backpack on one shoulder and a brown bag with bread under her opposite arm. That was all she had.

After tramping around several blocks, Martina found her new home. She did not complain about the spot. The house was right next to the Bladeking field, one of the few still vacant. *Maybe the area is too noisy, but I like it.* The princess thought the task was going to be easy. She closed her eyes and imagined a bed, a sofa, a table, everything she wanted for her new home. Instead, all she got was a twinge in her eyes. Her magic had gone awry. Martina had lost her powers.

Just then, the princess felt a weird sensation in her eyes again. They were getting dry. "Could it be the sea breeze?" Martina rubbed them with care. She tried to distract her mind. Maybe it was all a delusion, a false belief.

Martina sat at her front sandy door of the house. She pulled out her diary from the backpack. This time, it was gray. She read the latest poem, but she struggled to see the writing clearly.

She closed her diary and glanced at the word "calm" on the cover. There was no doubt that it described the life experience of people at Amo Island. But what could it mean to her? She tried to focus on the word, but the discomfort in her eyes worsened. It did not take long for Martina to bend down in pain. A sharp ache struck her eyes again.

Unexpectedly, a strong wind gust hit the backyard, and the gray diary rolled to the edge of a puddle, one of the obstacles in the Bladeking field.

Martina stretched across the floor to grasp the book. She breathed a sigh of relief as she lay on her back pressing the diary against her chest.

As she sat down, the princess looked at the book. It was pretty much unchanged. The same word was on the cover, but the color gray got a little bit darker. This time, Martina did not understand the message. Her diary was a riddle. Her mind was a riddle. Her heart was a riddle. Her life was a riddle. Nothing made sense except for one thing, the intense feeling of discomfort. The pain in her eyes had intensified.

Martina's gaze drifted up to the sky. Tears returned to her eyes. *Why? Why? As hard as I try, everything seems to go the wrong way.* She had never felt so hopeless in her life.

Castaway, Martina had gone into deep thoughts. She had lost her parents, her brother, her palace, and even worse, her magical powers. The only thing she thought was going well was the sand village, and now she could not even build a new house anymore. Martina felt all her efforts were worthless. "Nothing matters anymore! I may as well give up!" sobbed the princess.

CHAPTER EIGHTEEN

Back at Diamond Palace, King Drago continued with his abusive vision. The next oppressive move was soon to come.

At the throne room, King Drago announced a tax reform called the Brightax.

"Brightax is simply a newly imposed contribution to the revenue of the Brightalia Kingdom," explained King Drago.

A murmur was heard followed by total silence. The councilors exchanged baffled glances.

King Drago looked around and with a cynical smirk on his face, he added, "Every worker has to give fifty percent of his wage to the kingdom."

"Your Majesty, I believe it is an extremely high demand for our people. It will be unsustainable," said Lord Porto, stepping forward. "Farmers are already on the streets requesting their stands back at the Market."

"With all due respect, our economy is already impacted heavily. More drastic changes can only increase its instability," added Lord Campo from the back row.

"Excuse me!" roared King Drago, eyeing the councilors. "This is an informative assembly. Any suggestions or recommendations can be deposited at the burning box outside my office," said the king with a sarcastic voice. Drago rose from the throne and passed by the door, causing the guards to stand alert.

"If I may add, Your Majesty! I have a book that could enlighten your ruling with wisdom. Help you guide our kingdom in the right direction," suggested Lord Porto, trusting his many years as advisor of the kingdom.

"Enough!" shouted King Drago with a piercing gaze. His anger arose, and the echo of his voice traveled around the entire room. "I don't need your worthless book!"

"You're betraying the trust of your people!" shouted back the senior councilor.

The rest of the members remained still as statues disconcerted at the situation.

Immediately, two guards rushed to secure Lord Porto.

"Take him to the dungeons," barked King Drago, signaling the guards to get the councilor out of the room. "He is charged with treason."

"I know my way around the palace. They can escort me to the dungeons if there is still some respect left in this kingdom," said Lord Porto with dignity. He had been a loyal and devoted councilor serving the kingdom for many years. He had been the Prime Advisor to King Alessio's father. Now he was going to end up in an underground cell.

Drago hesitated, but then bobbed his head in agreement. The king did not miss the opportunity to intimidate the rest of the group. "Lord Porto is a traitor. He has betrayed our kingdom," said King Drago as he swaggered along the throne room.

A total hush enveloped the room.

"A high-level position has become vacant! Anyone interested? Any other suggestions?" the king asked with a sardonic smile.

Nobody answered.

"Well done, servants." King Drago left the room.

The introduction of the Brightax only worsened the already declining situation of the kingdom. King Drago proclaimed that money would be exclusively used to benefit the poor people. He made all kinds of attractive promises – better markets for the farmers, new plazas at the valley, and more schools for the children. And that was not all. His most audacious announcement was about Amo Island. King Drago took credit for the sand village. He claimed he had built it for his people, and now he had to use the Brightax money to pay for the construction.

In spite of the heavy demands on the pockets of every family, many still had confidence in the good faith of their kingdom's ruler. They were used to King Alessio, who always had been responsive to the needs of his people and never deceived them.

Obviously, King Drago did not deliver on any of his promises. It was all lies. He did not spend a single coin for the welfare of his people or for the improvement and development of the kingdom. All the wealth stayed at Diamond Palace. Gold was pouring into his coffers like rain showers. Servants were outraged at the squandering of money on luxurious sculptures and extravagant art pieces decorating the palace.

The palace became an art museum. Its new color was gold. However, it looked dull and desolate. It was never illuminated after Drago assumed the throne.

King Drago was enjoying all his outrageous accomplishments. Every night, he delighted himself with exquisite banquets of food and then empowered his mind reading and playing the piano in the music room.

King Drago was convinced that he was taking the right path

for his future and his kingdom. But that night, a peculiar event happened. When he got to his room, he found a handwritten note on his bed. It read: *Wealth is not based on how much you own, but the treasures held inside you.*

Drago was really curious about the note. He had no idea where the message came from. He asked the servants at the palace, but he never got an answer.

King Drago ordered General Althar to investigate the origin of the mysterious note. Drago trusted Althar and was confident that the general would do anything he commanded. He was very different from his father. King Alessio had his reservations about the general and kept him always under close radar. He never liked the fact that Althar did not look at him straight in his eyes.

"So where is the fancy note coming from?" asked the king impatiently. Drago sat at his royal desk in the Diamond Office. He watched Althar while moving a pen between his fingers.

"Your Majesty, one of my sergeants recognized the handwriting. He tells me an old man from the sand village is the messenger," General Althar said with confidence.

"An old man? What in the world does an old man want from me?" puzzled King Drago.

"He's really an old wizard," clarified the general, fixing his cap. "Maybe he's trying to imply that you need to pay closer attention to the way you're ruling the kingdom," General Althar did not like the look that he received back from the king. "Just a guess!" Althar added.

The pen flew out of the king's hand and hit the window behind his chair. "We have a new candidate for the dungeons." King Drago rubbed his chin, lifting his right eyebrow.

"How soon do you want him here?" asked General Althar, reaching for another pen to hand to the king. But as he leaned forward, a notebook felt out of his pocket. It was one of Martina's notepads.

King Drago frowned, looking at the purple book. "What is that?"

"Helping my daughter with school work!" uttered the general rather quickly. He squashed the small notebook inside his pocket in no time. Then he flung himself onto a chair pretending he was tired. "So, should I get my hands on the wizard?"

"You bet!" said King Drago still staring at the navy jacket of the Chief of Army. "Two days is all you have." He held up two fingers.

The kingdom was crying for help. Suffering had arrived in Brightalia. The Brightax was destroying the lives of the Brightalians.

There was light at the Diamond Palace, but darkness at Enna Valley. Illuminated and colorful streets changed to desolate and dirty roads. Hard working and contented shopkeepers became scared and monitored villagers. Happy and cheerful kids turned into wretched and lonely children.

Scarcity was around every corner. Some merchants rode to the border to trade any goods they had for food. Others remained on the streets protesting. It seemed as if Brightalia had gone back a thousand years, the same time of the evil ruler. There was nothing to eat. Villagers were starving!

Tons of people arrived at Amo Island in desperate need of a new home. Martina did her best to accommodate everybody, but soon the houses on the island ran out. A few children stayed at her house. She was living and feeling the pain of her people. She also thought about her poor friend Enzo. She hoped he had survived the situation and wished he would stop by one day. But it was Mercy who paid a visit to Martina. The nanny, who had become the new spy at the palace, went to Amo Island looking for the princess. She told Martina all about Drago's cruel ruling and his outrageous lies. The nanny updated Martina on the farmland problem. Castella continued pressing at Lusha's borders, and Brightalia's troops struggled to push the enemies back.

Before heading back to Enna Valley, Mercy also advised Martina about the ancient wizard. The princess wondered who the old man was. She did not know a Master Wizard lived in the sand village. She needed to find the old man. Maybe he could help the kingdom. She told Mercy she had lost her power, and she could do nothing to save Brightalia.

CHAPTER NINETEEN

K ing Drago continued, blind to his doctrines. His ambition to rule, to have power, and to control his people did not allow him to see the chaos he was creating. Brightalia was falling down. The kingdom was on the brink of war.

King Drago kept pressing the Council to follow his commands, control all the food distribution, and levy the Brightax.

The village had to obey all the new arbitrary regulations. It was true that their voices began to be heard, louder and louder every day. Yet King Drago was not ready to stop. He just gave a different twist to his malevolent ruling. Where was he going next? To a controversial place!

Inside Diamond Office, a map of Lusha Land lay flat on a table.

"We'll redistribute all farmlands and give small acre plots to those in need. Then we will plant in the available lands," said King Drago, standing next to the long rectangular table.

"Your Majesty!" The Emissary to Land Resources wrinkled his nose as he peered at the map trying to understand what the king wanted. "I understand the farming problem, but we cannot arbitrarily take the empty lands," Lord Campo said with a brooding look. He pulled out a handkerchief from under his burgundy robe and cleaned his round glasses.

"Let's just say that as of today all cultivated and uncultivated lands in Lusha belongs to the kingdom." King Drago extended his hand, gliding over the map. "That means I have the authority to distribute the lands as I please," the king told the emissary sternly. He walked to the end of the table and resting his hands on the edge, he added, "Sounds like a great plan to me. Everybody will love me!"

"You know there are Castellian soldiers at the border, threatening war. Are you sure of what you are doing?" asked Lord Campo with sweating hands. He could not swallow what the king had ordered. But he was afraid of opposing his request. He had a family of his own and did not want to end up in the dungeon. He thought about the councilors who were prisoners in cells without committing any crime. The emissary strove for a different destiny.

The king nodded. "Totally convinced! And don't worry about help. General Althar will support the operation," said King Drago, tapping Lord Campo on his shoulder.

"I heard my name," General Althar showed at the door.

"Come in Althar. I'm sharing the Lusha Land Expansion Plan with Lord Campo." King Drago got a roll-up map from the general.

"The strategy map is ready. I can send my regiment as soon as you give us the green light." General Althar walked toward the table.

"The Expansion Plan?" the emissary whispered between his teeth. His glasses flashed as he studied the map one more time.

"Better sooner than later! You can start tonight," said Drago, unrolling the strategy map. "A threatening plan is what we need! Get there by surprise." The king shot a baleful glance at the general.

"I have selected our highly experienced squadrons to assemble this regiment. They just completed an advanced crossbow training and a hiking fitness program the previous week," said the general proudly. "They can build a Command Center in no time."

"A Command Center?" murmured Lord Campo, shaking his head in total disbelief.

"Very important topic!" King Drago directed his gaze at the map. "Acardi owned the largest ranch in the area," the king pointed out. "Establish our Command Center here." King Drago traced a circle around the coffee ranch.

"As you order, Your Majesty," responded General Althar with a military salute.

Lord Campo remained silent this time.

"Oh, before I forget!" added General Althar. "I have a letter for Your Majesty." He approached the king. "The Emissary from Castella came this morning to deliver this invitation," added General Althar, handing the envelope to King Drago.

"What does Falco want this time?" The king tore up one end of the envelope. "Didn't I prohibit his access to the palace?"

"Your Majesty, the main guards at the front gates did not allow Lord Falco to enter the palace. They received the invitation and handed it to me," explained the general.

"I don't need any invitation from Castella!" King Drago opened the letter with rage.

"Your Majesty, it must be the letter to attend the Castella Assembly, the follow-up summit conference to address the Lusha Land dispute," informed Lord Campo with a flat voice. "Why don't you go first to the meeting before implementing your Expansion Plan?"

The king ripped apart the letter into small pieces, crushed

the pieces together, and tossed the paper ball out the window. "Assembly concluded! I will never sign a document to grant me ownership of my own lands. The claimed territory will not be deserted any longer. I'll build there now. Brightalia will remember me as the farming king!"

"Your Majesty, I don't want to interfere in your decisions, but I don't think this plan is a good idea. We can save our land peaceably. We just need to be patient and wait a little bit longer." Lord Campo finally dared to say something.

"We won't wait another day. It is my time, Campo ... the perfect time!" King Drago responded with a strong voice.

Lord Campo stared at the strategy map with concern. "I foresee difficult times at Lusha Land," muttered the emissary in a low voice.

"What did you just say?" King Drago looked straight at Lord Campo.

Lord Campo turned to the King with hesitation. He could not ignore his obligation to the kingdom. "Your decision is absolutely respected, Your Majesty, but please understand that it is my duty to recommend that you attend the assembly meeting. We have made great progress, and we should not take the risk of unleashing unnecessary fights. A war will erupt as soon as Castella finds out your Expansion Plan," advised the emissary.

"Castella will never take Lusha," affirmed King Drago, striking his fist on the table. His face felt warm. "Pulverize the bones of any Castellian in our lands! Burn all the rebels!" said King Drago, raising his authoritarian voice.

The initial expansion plan was certainly executed. The Brightalian army gained total control of the existing plantations and redistributed those lands as the king ordered. Nonetheless, the result was not fruitful. The new farm owners did not know how to plant a seed. They had some land, but the crops lost their experienced hands. The expert peasants were already expecting their first harvest in Amo Island.

King Drago was at the peak of his own mountain. He celebrated his new accomplishment with a feast. All military personnel attended the lunch event organized by General Althar. Acardi's extensive field housed the celebration. King Drago offered a succinct speech in gratitude for the military support during the expansion plan. The operation was a success to his eyes. The king recalled when his dad used to ignore his suggestions. Now he enjoyed the authority to implement them.

What else could King Drago impose on his people to prove his power?

CHAPTER TWENTY

Months of suffering clouded the rich farmlands. Newcomers struggled to cultivate the fields. The livestock were dying. They could not earn any money. Many tears ran along those fields. Surviving was getting more complicated in the farmlands every day.

King Drago did not listen to Lord Campo's advice. He did not attend the Castella Assembly meeting. The two kingdoms did not sign the agreement. Lushers were still waiting for the new promised houses at the farms. But King Drago did not want to let the gold out of his coffers. Instead, he ordered the establishment of military tents in the claimed area. Peasants were sent off to occupy the free lands. Soldiers spent their time guarding the northern border with Castella. The great expansion plan was put to the big test.

Filippo, the heir to the throne and new King of Castella, immediately reacted to the situation. Brightalia had broken all the rules. It was time to declare war! Castella was ready to fight not for a part, but for the entire Lusha Land as well. A great source of income for his modest kingdom had been placed in his hands. Filippo would not miss that opportunity. His huge army strategically hid in a concealed position waiting for the perfect time to strike.

General Althar rushed inside the Diamond Office, slamming the door open. "Your Majesty, Castella attacked our border troops," gasped the general with empty lungs.

Lord Campo followed behind with round eyes. He was the perfect shadow of General Althar.

King Drago stood. He was fuming, and his face turned red. "How in the world did this happen?" yelled the king, walked sullenly toward the map table.

"King Filippo ambushed our border troops when they started the night patrol," said General Althar with a pale face.

"Our soldiers were killed, and Castellian troops are furiously penetrating Lusha Land. They are burning our fields," explained Lord Campo. He could barely move. His voice quivered.

"Started the night patrol? Where were they before?" shouted King Drago. He struck his fist straight at the Lusha-Castella border on the map.

"I had called them for a brief meeting." The general gave an apologetic look to the king.

"Enough! No excuses! You assured and reassured that this would never happen!" scolded King Drago. He crushed the map hard between his fingers, letting all his fury out.

King Drago could not stand the possibility of being defeated. "Send our entire army, every sergeant, every soldier, every villager if necessary!" ordered the king with a firm voice.

"Immediately, Your Majesty," responded General Althar. He headed back to the door at a brisk pace.

"I haven't finished!" barked the king. He walked to the general and poked a stiff finger at his chest. "Assassins are not welcomed to my land. Eliminate every single Castellian soldier in or close to Lusha Land. Understood?" finished King Drago, twisting the general's uniform.

"Yes, Your Majesty!" The general saluted the king and then straightened his jacket.

Lord Campo remained in the room. He smoothed the map and studied the attacked area. "Your Majesty, I know Lusha better than my own house – every ranch, every field, and every hidden rock. If I may propose a plan, a strategic plan that—" Lord Campo began explaining, but the king quickly interrupted him.

"There is no time for planning. The only plan here is to destroy Castella. Raze all buildings to the ground." King Drago turned his eyes to the emissary.

Lady Zirry showed at the door. "I apologize for my unannounced arrival, but urgent medical assistance is crucial at Lusha Land. Many are seriously wounded. Kids cry searching for their parents. It is devastating," the Councilor of Health spoke quickly as she entered the room. She wore her usual scarlet robe.

Lord Campo sat and gave his stiff back a quick rub. "This situation is so sad," the councilor murmured, nodding his head. He knew the king was only listening to himself.

King Drago just stretched his neck. His eyes aimed at the Councilor of Health.

At the unexpected silence, Lady Zirry added, "I'm just trying to help our people. Lusha Land is in flames. It's our responsibility to protect and save them." Lady Zirry begged with desperate urgency to provide medical personnel and supplies.

King Drago could not see beyond his selfish world. His anger and his thirst for power were turning him into the real assassin. "My need is to show Filippo who is the true king here," said

King Drago, pointing at the map. "Time for revenge!" King Drago laughed out loud.

Lady Zirry's mouth opened in bewilderment. "Your Majesty, our people are dying! Let me send a rescue and assistance commission," insisted the councilor.

"I don't want to hear another word!" shouted the king. "Do whatever you want, but get out of my sight!"

Lord Campo stood and left the room shaking his head. Lady Zirry rushed after the emissary.

"Filippo will never forget Drago I." Drago ripped apart the map with wild fury. His eyes projected his uncontrollable anger. "I won't rest until I crumble Castella into nothing," screamed the king at the top of his lungs. The walls of the palace shook echoing Drago's words.

A long silence shadowed the following weeks. Those were the toughest days for Brightalia. King Drago's anger turned into frustration. For once in his life, he felt powerless. A cloud of confusion shuttered the king's mind. Somebody else had shaken his ground. The battle continued and the kingdom was tumbling.

King Drago feared to lose his total control. In the turquoise dining room, he could not swallow a bite of food or take a sip of water. That night, the king went searching for the light to continue his cruel road.

He read his inseparable red book, but to his annoyance, another mysterious note appeared right in front of his eyes. The handwritten paper said: *Land is a gift for everybody. Nurse it, embrace it, and share it with your neighbors.* How could the messages be so in line with the kingdom's situation? This time, there was not a chance for the king to ignore the old wizard. "I want that intruder writer here!" King Drago furiously barked.

Early the next morning, General Althar was on his way to receive a new task. King Drago waited impatiently in the library room.

"What am I good for, Your Majesty?" asked General Althar as he entered the library.

King Drago approached the main bookcase, and rubbing his hand along some books, he said, "Do you remember when we talked about the famous wizard at the sand village?"

The general nodded. "Of course! The Master Wizard!"

"What are you waiting for to capture him?" growled the king. His face was darker than the scarlet robe of Lady Zirry.

"My apologies, Your Majesty! All my resources have been tied up at Lusha. It has been our greatest army deployment, and I have to admit that my focus was diverted away from the arrest." The general managed to find a good excuse, one that the king surprisingly did not refute.

"I want the wizard at the dungeons, no later than tomorrow." The King tapped a book with his stiff finger.

"He'll be in prison tomorrow. We will knock on every door if necessary," confirmed the general with a rough voice. This time, Althar knew he had to deliver on his promise. He emphasized one more time, "I'll get him myself."

The king beamed broadly. He sat on a sofa. "Give me an update on the Lusha War," said the king, leaning forward.

General Althar coughed a couple of times to clear his throat. "The fights continue in Lusha. Castella had sent more troops. We're doing our best. But it has been a challenge to control the fires. A lot of the fields have been lost. The land is still burning. The only untouched areas are the extensions bordering the stream, the south part of Lusha."

"How far in Castella are our troops? I want to smell their flames and see their ashes!" King Drago swaggered to a tall flowerpot. He squeezed some sand in his hand and let it fall to the floor slowly.

"Almost inland, Your Majesty," responded the general, staring at the sand.

"Almost? And what about Filippo's castle?" said the king with a cynical look.

"We're working on the plan. It's not an easy target." The general crushed the sand on the floor with his foot. "Filippo's castle will look just like this sand."

King Drago let out one of his loud, silly laughs.

Suddenly, General Althar's face grew serious. "There is something else I must tell you."

"Go ahead," said King Drago, kicking the sand to the side.

"You know many Lushers have left for Amo Island. I hear it has become a very nice and peaceful place to live." The general walked in circles.

"Althar, speak your mind fast! What are you trying to say?" King Drago demanded, losing his patience. "Stop walking like a dog trying to catch its tail!" The king pointed at a sofa for the general to sit.

General Althar sat and sighed. "Reliable sources have informed me that the sand village was created by..." the general paused.

"By whom?" shouted King Drago. He looked straight at the general. "Finish Althar, finish!"

"By your sister, Your Majesty," answered General Althar. "People are very happy with her." The general knew that King Drago would not like the threatening news.

"Martina!" roared the king. The truth was out and well

spread. "Is she the new leader our people want?" The king gave a mocking laugh.

General Althar's face remained grave. "I wish I don't have to say this ... but yes! And no offense, it's a marvelous place. People seem to be loyal to her."

"Impossible!" opposed King Drago. Blood rushed to his face. "My sister will never take away my throne." He pushed a chair to the side and moved close to a window. "This is the last thing I need to hear!" He looked outside. Then he returned to the sofa and stopped behind General Althar. "I want Martina in our darkest cell," whispered the king in the general's ear.

Drago rested his hands on Althar's shoulders, pressing down on the general's uniform. He walked to the side of the sofa and narrowed his eyes at the Chief of Army. "Even if you have to battle the biggest storm, I want my sister here tomorrow. My sister and the dead wizard!" screamed King Drago with a wild look on his face. "Did I make myself clear?"

"Clear as the water!" General Althar rose from the couch. He put on his cap and added, "It'll be my pleasure. They will be here sooner than you imagine." The general smiled and exited the library room.

"You better Althar, you better!" King Drago stomped off down the hallway in the opposite direction.

CHAPTER TWENTY-ONE

The Castellian army was making good ground. They were taking over the Lusha territory and quickly advancing into their neighboring kingdom. Enzo, who had worked his back off to find food for his mom and him, had just lost his house. Soldiers from Castella invaded the small cottage, forcing them to leave. He had no choice but to take his weak mother to a medical emergency tent.

A nurse walked along the aisles of stretchers delivering water and two measly remedies for the sick. Julia rested at the last cot to the right. Enzo stood beside her. The scene was not a happy one.

"Stay with me, Mom," said Enzo in a grim voice. The woman's skin was so thin that Enzo could see all the veins and feel every skeletal bone.

"Son, there's something you must know," said Julia in her frail voice. "Your dad—" She sighed, feeling the tightness in her chest. She could barely keep her pink eyes opened. The yellow spots on her eyelids were not a promising sign.

"You need to rest." Enzo lifted his mom's head slightly to allow her to take a sip of water. He could see the sadness in his mom's pale face. For years, he had tried his best to take care of his sick mom and find the food and remedies she needed.

"You're special, son." Julia coughed, gasping for air. A second or twenty more passed by. Then she added, "And I want to tell you why." But her wispy voice was almost gone, same as her white hair. Everything had become difficult. She could not move her feeble body.

Enzo's heart sank. He knew the moment was coming. "I love you, Mom!" He softly wrapped his arms around Julia. His eyes welled up with tears. He had nobody else, but his mom. He did not want to lose her.

"Love you more." The woman turned her head, and making a painful effort, she kissed the top of her son's head.

The light seemed to dim. The sound appeared to have been sucked up by the air.

"Mom! Please don't leave me!" cried Enzo. He clung to his mom's body.

"Enzo … you … the truth is—" One last breath, and Julia's eyes closed forever. Famine had taken her life.

"*Nooo!*" screamed Enzo, breaking into inconsolable sobs. "Please someone help me!" The lonely peasant buried his head in his mom's chest and hugged her cold and lanky body. It seemed as though his world had stopped revolving. He wished he could turn time back. But it was too late. His mother was gone!

A crowd gathered around the soon empty cot.

With tears still in his eyes, Enzo went looking for a place to stay. He decided to visit his friend, Martina. As he crossed Enna Valley, his heart felt a deep pain at the desolation and devastation of Brightalia.

Just as Enzo arrived at Amo Island, everything changed. He felt an inner peace. It was impressive how the sand island transmitted so much tranquility. It was hard to understand how two places so close to each other could be at the same time so far apart and different.

Enzo got to the pier while looking for Martina. When he reached the end, he turned around and admired the sand village. He was amazed! The charm and freshness of Martina were stamped in every gain of sand. *How can the ruling of one person make the life of many so miserable or pleasurable?* Enzo wondered. He sat on a bench deeply thinking about life and his future. Then, he saw a group of kids playing on the shore and asked them for Martina.

"I can take you to her house," said a young blonde girl. "I know exactly where she lives."

"Great!" Enzo recovered a pinch of happiness. "My name is Enzo," he said, and that was the beginning of his fishing story.

They both ambled down the sandy streets. They took a slow stroll through the small market, and later they circled around the Sand Plaza. As they finally got close to the house, the girl told Enzo something that warned his ears, something that darkened the nice tour.

"Did you know that the princess lost her powers?" The young kid kept sauntering down the road.

"What?" Enzo halted mid-step. "Are you a hundred percent sure?"

The girl turned and added quite naturally, "Yes, King Drago hurt her eyes!"

"No!" Enzo groaned. "Drago must stop. Now!" It was unbelievable the madness that he had caused to the entire kingdom. Enzo counted the injustices one by one – villagers at Enna Valley were starving. Innocent people were in prisons. New farmers had no idea what to do with their lands. The claimed territory was in flames. Soldiers were dying upon the Lusha border. To top that, Enzo could add his own list. The poor peasant had battled every unfair reform, lost his home, and suffered the death of his mother. Just when he thought the bad news could be over, he found out that Drago had hurt his own sister, the one person who was helping Brightalia. Somebody had to do something.

Enzo thanked the girl and walked out, never getting to Martina's house. Enraged, he snorted, "I'll stop Drago!" He headed back to Enna Valley. Diamond Palace was his next stop. Enzo was ready to fight, and this time, it was not at a Bladeking field! He was determined to force King Drago to step down from the throne at any cost. Brightalia needed a good ruler, like Martina.

Meanwhile, Princess Martina was at a remote end of Amo Island. She had struggled for weeks to accommodate every new farmer at the sand village. Her own house had been transformed into a foster home. Martina turned to the open water and headed to the farthest house in the village. It helped only to confirm that the house was not empty. One curious detail was that nobody had planted a single seed in that back yard.

Suddenly, her hands warmed. She was holding her diary. The charmed book had not shown any activity lately. In fact, Martina had been using it as a notepad to track the houses available. The princess stopped suddenly and looked at the now red book. It did not show a word on the cover, but it felt hot. She quickly opened the diary to the last page. A colored drawing appeared. Martina had never seen colors inside the diary before. The page showed the secret view of the West tower, but fires surrounded Lusha Land.

Martina's heart lurched when she remembered her mom's words: "Flames arriving at one of the unique views of the palace can mark the end of our kingdom." *Lusha is one of the views. Is the prediction of the ancient wizards true?* She paled at the thought. With shaky hands, the princess snapped the red diary shut and darted away from the remote house. But she bumped into an old man.

"I'm so sorry, sir! Are you okay?" Martina reached down, grabbed a staff from the ground, and handed it to the old man. She was still trying to recover the rosiness in her face.

The old man kept inching slowly until his silver stick touched the steps of a porch. It was the remote house that Martina had just checked to see if it was available. Resting on a side wall was a green canoe.

With shiny bald head and silver long beard, the old man sat on the porch. It seemed as if he were waiting for Martina. "My dearest princess," said the man with a weak voice. "Please, come here!" He waved his trembling hand at Martina.

The princess got close to the old man. He wore a long white tunic with a wide stole around his neck. Brown sandals covered his wrinkled feet. The man raised his hands to touch Martina's hair and face. "You are a beautiful lady, my princess. Your delicate face is softer than a rose petal," said the old man.

"Thank you, sir," responded Martina. She observed the old man tapping his metal staff between his feet. Then a memory from her childhood surfaced. *These are the same old leather sandals that saved me from the ralthors! And the same old guy who gave me a prophecy at the beach.* Martina's eyes glowed.

"My name is Fabrizio, but you can call me Dr. Brizio," added the old man.

"Dr. Brizio? Are ... are you a wizard?" asked Martina with excitement.

The old man beamed, but he did not answer.

Martina hesitated. She was unsure of what to say or ask. "Do you want to take a walk with me?" Martina finally suggested.

"I would be delighted, my princess. There are some things I need to share with you," said the old man.

Martina helped Fabrizio stand up, and they commenced a long walk down the road to the Sand Plaza.

Dr. Brizio started telling Martina about his old days at the kingdom. It was better than reading any book about the history of Brightalia. The old man told her how a dark wizard created terror in the kingdom a thousand years ago.

Martina listened carefully.

Dr. Brizio was adding all the flavor to the story, including the coronation of Drago as King of Brightalia.

"It was an unexpected and sudden twist that marked the history of our kingdom," said Dr. Brizio, aiding his walk with the staff.

The more they walked, the sadder the book was becoming. Dr. Brizio knew that it was time to cease the suffering and begin the rebirth of the kingdom.

The old man stopped suddenly. Putting his hand on Martina's shoulder, he said, "My lovely princess, don't forget your mission. You must rescue Brightalia! Your brother has immersed the kingdom in a world of oppression, suffering, and scarcity. The kingdom is collapsing in flames."

Martina felt a strong knot clenching her gut. "But ... but I cannot fight my brother," she stammered.

"But you can rescue him. He has learned the black magic of the wizardry book."

Martina's eyes widened. "You mean the red book is the dark book of magic?" She felt somewhat scared.

"Yes!" Fabrizio nodded. "The one your brother refuses to

show anyone."

"If only I could recover my magical powers," Martina said sadly. Her eyes filled up with tears.

Fabrizio remained silent.

"Who are you? Please tell me! Are you a wizard?" insisted Martina.

Fabrizio looked up. "Yes, Martina. I am a Royal Wizard of Brightalia, one of the creators of the Red Sagerant or red book as you call it."

"You are?" Martina felt a rush of emotion running through her veins. She did not know if she was feeling happy or afraid. Yet she clearly knew she was about to understand the past of her kingdom. "Please, tell me what happened."

Master Fabrizio smiled. "Let's start from the beginning." The old man rubbed his long beard. He explained that the Sagerant was an ancient wizardry book filled with key messages about the past, present, and future of Brightalia. Nobody could dispute that the red book gave wisdom to the land rulers, until one day a dark wizard stole the book and added all his black magic to it. Everybody became terrified about magic, and no one believed in the Sagerant anymore. "Since then, I've been living on this island in disguise, waiting for the day the book reappeared."

By then, Martina and Fabrizio had made it to the Sand Plaza. They sat on a bench.

Martina felt as though she were attending a crash course in Brightalia history.

The royal wizard placed his hands together around the staff. He turned his head to the princess. "Martina, Drago's dark powers are massive. You must find the Sagerant and burn it before it is too late. Once the red book is destroyed, all of Drago's black magic knowledge will be erased from his memory," the old wizard advised without hesitation.

"Please help me recover my powers. I know you can do it," Martina sobbed. She held the old man's hand in a tight grip. It was not easy what Dr. Brizio was asking of her.

The old man gently cleaned Martina's tears. "First you must believe in yourself again. You have been hopeless and abandoned your mission to save Brightalia. Your kingdom needs you," affirmed Master Fabrizio in a warning voice.

Martina was speechless. She felt as if a bucket of ice had been dumped on top of her for not doing what she was supposed to. "I am so sorry," she admitted, covering her face with her hands. "I should never give up."

Dr. Brizio gently grabbed Martina's chin with his weak hand and turned her face to him. "Your powers are still inside you. You must try harder." Then, Dr. Brizio pointed his finger at Martina's heart. "A love sacrifice can restore your powers."

"A love sacrifice?" repeated Martina. "If I destroy the red book to save my brother that will be the perfect love sacrifice! Then I will recover my power and help rebuild Brightalia." Martina was convinced she had all the answers she needed.

"It's not quite right, but I'm sure you'll get there," Fabrizio smiled.

Martina's eyes shone with happiness.

"Well, I must go now. You're running out of time, Martina," alerted Dr. Brizio.

"I can't thank you enough, Master Wizard. I must dream big for Brightalia!" said Martina with an energetic voice, remembering Enzo's words. "It is time to save my kingdom."

"That's the Martina I needed to hear." The royal wizard stood, raised his hands over the princess's head, and said some weird words.

"May I accompany you back to your house?" asked Martina.

"I know this sand village like the palm of my hand," responded

Fabrizio. He turned his back on Martina and started his slow walk back home. "Come back and visit me," said the old man with a soft voice.

"I will, Dr. Brizio!"

Back at her house, Martina observed how her magical diary darkened into a black color again. The word "power" appeared on top of the key outline.

Martina tried to make some sense of the meaning. Was it referring to the absolute power Drago was imposing on Brightalia? Or maybe was it alluding to Drago's dark powers? One thing was clear in Martina's mind. She was determined to rescue her confused brother no matter how challenging that could be.

Martina was ready to return to Diamond Palace. At that instant, an unexpected hand squeezed her arm. Every natural movement disappeared from her body. She could not move a muscle. She only felt the adrenalin flowing through her veins.

"General Althar!" sighed Martina, pressing her other hand to her chest. Her heartbeats accelerated like a fast train.

"The person I needed to find," the general grinned. "King Drago ordered your arrest," said General Althar with a rough voice. He let go Martina's arm and trooped to an open window.

"Please, General, I cannot be imprisoned right now! I must save—"

The general turned to Martina. "And who said I will apprehend you?" Althar cut her off. He walked close to Martina, extending his arm to the princess.

"You are not?" asked Martina with a confused face. No doubt, she also felt some relief. Martina walked to the front door of the house.

"No, Your Highness! But time is running out," said the general looking directly into Martina's eyes. "I knew you had sent some notes to your brother. This notepad, where you practiced your handwriting, helped me to identify that the messages came from you." Althar gave the princess her purple notebook. "I've been trying to protect you, but it's not easy to fool King Drago." Although the general liked Drago's aggressiveness at making decisions, he now realized they were always the wrong choices.

"Brightalia will rise again," confirmed Martina, grabbing her notepad. She did not want to tell the truth to protect her nanny, but Martina knew that Mercy was the one sending the notes and imitating her writing. Sad to say, her attempts to try to make Drago change his mind were fruitless.

The visit was very quick. "One more thing," Althar said, sliding his foot up into the stirrup of his horse. "I found out a wizard lives here. Maybe he can help you." And he was gone.

Martina just waved good-bye. The news was old, but the princess was glad the general was on her side.

Just after Althar left, the blonde girl showed up at the door. "Martina, Martina," called the kid, pulling the princess's arm down to reach her ear.

Martina bent forward and asked, "What is it?" The fuchsia eyes of the girl revealed some urgency.

"Somebody is going to fight your brother," she hissed. The girl had come running when she saw the princess. "He left not too long ago."

"Who is he?" Martina asked filled with curiosity. None came to her mind.

"En…" The girl thought for a moment. Then the name came out. "Enzo! His name is Enzo."

"Enzo?" repeated Martina. Her hands flew to her head. She had to return to the palace to stop Enzo from killing her brother or getting killed. Enzo had no idea Drago's dark powers had grown massively.

In a bind, Martina jumped onto White Diamond and rode out of the sand island. There was no time to look for the red book. Martina was going to have to face her brother and convince him to stop the madness. Would she make it on time?

CHAPTER TWENTY-TWO

It was an unnatural nightfall at Brightalia, a moonless night. Gray iron clouds covered the dense sky from Lusha Land to Enna Valley. The wind picked up as Enzo arrived at Diamond Palace.

An unprecedented storm was approaching. Brilliant flashes of light ran like snakes in the inky sky. The loud sound of thunder quivered throughout the kingdom. Heavy rain beat houses and windows, and shallow rivers ran along the streets and farming fields.

Prince Drago ordered the servants to close all windows at Diamond Palace. He went to the music room and started playing his piano. The rain kept crashing the windows with no end. The harder Drago hit the keys on his piano, the more intense the rain became. King Drago kept playing his discordant melody faster and harder. But the music could barely be heard over the high wind.

Opening the door in one blow, Enzo stepped inside the music room. "I finally find you, Mr. Tyrant!" The peasant was soaked by the rain. His broken boots exposed his muddy toes.

King Drago hit the last key and turned around. "Oh!

Fish-face," laughed Drago, looking at the mucky appearance of Enzo. "How did you get here?"

Enzo attempted to dry his face with the sleeve of his wet shirt. "I still remember my way in through the stables." He looked at the window as another flash of electrifying lightning etched the sky.

Drago stood and approached Enzo. "And what brings you here?" He went ahead and answered his own question with a mocking smile. "An umbrella? I have plenty!" The king paused for a few seconds. "Because…" He walked around Enzo, pretending to be thinking. Then he added raising his authoritarian voice, "Because there is nothing else you need to do in my palace!"

"Yes, there is," replied Enzo with a shout. "You don't deserve this palace. You don't deserve the Brightalia throne. You're nothing more than a phony king." His face was uncomfortably close to that of Drago. "You betrayed your kingdom and hurt your own sister. What else is still left for you to do?"

King Drago cracked his neck, and his expression turned very dark. "Kill any inferior who dares to question my rule!" roared Drago with wild eyes. His face lit up like a wood-burning oven. "You're a dead man tonight!"

"And you're a mercenary," Enzo said fiercely. He needed to somehow let out all the sorrow and suffering he carried inside regardless of the consequences. Right then, the brave peasant put all his strength into a punch that hit the king right in his mouth.

Taken by surprise, King Drago fell on his back on the floor. He touched his lips with one hand, later with his tongue. The king could taste a drop of blood in his mouth, bitter and salty. Drago was angrier than a raging black lion. He could not bear the audacity of Enzo. "You'll know who I really am right now!"

Drago's evil laughter echoed around the room as he climbed back to his feet. At once, the frenzied king pointed his hands at the ground. They released some type of blue light similar to sparks of electricity. The floor started to crumble. The opening crack snaked straight at Enzo, chewing a long animal rug as if a vacuum were below the ground. Smoke wafted from the long narrow hole and twirled around the room.

Enzo jumped to one side of the crack, right before falling down. "You're a monster!"

"Enzo!" said a panting voice.

The peasant took a quick peek at the door. "What are you doing here?"

"Leave now!" Martina screamed at Enzo, skidding her way into the room. She glanced quickly around the disastrous place. Suddenly, loud thunder seemed to boom in the palace. The princess tried to swallow, but her throat was completely dry. Her head spun in a daze. *Is this really happening?* This time, the palace rumbled even stronger ending with a loud bang. *Yes, it is!* Martina finally realized. The first image that came to her mind was that of her mom. How many times did Queen Constanza try to keep Martina away from magic? Now, the princess was face to face with the dark force, her own brother. She was scared but mostly sad.

"Join the party!" barked Drago. His voice sounded ghoulish. "I can kill two birds with one stone." At that instant, Drago transformed himself into a powerful monster. His blue eyes turned bright yellow, and one white, lazy eye appeared on his forehead. Long arms also grew on his back, ripping off his black robe. The king stretched the new dorsal tentacles to touch Martina's face. The two good eyes looked at her. "This kingdom belongs to me."

The scene was terrifying, and Martina was even more aghast.

The nasty arms wrapped around her neck. "I don't know you anymore," wept Martina with her strangled voice. She pulled hard on the slippery tentacles, trying to free herself. But Drago raised her into the air. The murderous limbs tightened around her neck.

"Leave her alone. Your fight is with me," yelled Enzo. He picked up a flanged mace from a knight armor sculpture and moved into a desperate attack. He swung his weapon straight at Drago, beating him hard in the stomach multiple times.

"You're so weak. You can't fight this battle," guffawed Drago without even a tiny flinch of pain. He spread one of his tentacles and propelled the peasant into the air.

Enzo crashed on top of a table. He did not have time to realize that the landing was not going to be smooth. The desk cracked into pieces sending Enzo hard to the floor. The poor villager ended up covered with rubble. A rough touchdown!

The evil king glared at Martina. His now filthy teeth parked right at her nose. His grin was disgusting and malodorous. It smelled like rotting cheese. The grave and deep voice of Drago spoke again, "No one can save you, Martina! Surrender to me, and I will spare your friend." His tongue stuck out like a kite in the wind.

In panic, Martina continued gasping for air. But her lungs were empty. Her brother was choking her. Heartbroken, Martina realized she had to fight Drago. She needed to win this dark battle. The princess gave a sudden jerk of her head and dug her nails forcefully into the tentacles until she was able to pull them apart. A spray of goo burst from the long limbs. The tentacles broke and unwrapped abruptly. Martina rolled down to the floor. Her legs hung down to the crack, but Enzo grabbed her hand, just in time for Martina to stay in place.

Still dazed from the blow, Enzo turned to Drago. "Let your

sister leave and kill me," said the brave peasant with a firm voice. Bumbling, he staggered toward Drago, protecting his body with a metal shield from the armor.

King Drago also prowled closer to Enzo. He smashed his own desk with his broken tentacles. Pieces of wood scattered even to the main corridor. "Nobody is gonna stand in my way. Your destiny is death," he snorted. Red flames curled out from his mouth. The fire burst across the room and melted an entire wall of bookcases, quickly turning them to ashes. The long draperies blazed like a bonfire. One of the whirling flames brushed Enzo's arm.

"Ouch!" cried Enzo. The tormented look on his face revealed the sharp burning pain of his skin. But he was ready to die for Martina.

The room turned pitch-dark and hot. The cracks climbed up the walls like ivy, and the ceiling began to break apart.

King Drago opened his mouth and launched fireballs at his victims, just like a dragon. As the glowing balls hit the floor, they turned into red-hot lava that quickly spread around.

A few of the sizzling balls caught the princess. Her blood rushed to her feet, and her pale face could not hide her dizziness. She was about to faint. Martina doubled over in pain. She was trapped between two walls. She made an effort not to lose her wits. She knew she had to remain focused and be brave.

"Are you okay?" Enzo hurtled in front of Martina to protect her. "Stay back there." He advised the princess. Tentacles, arcs of electricity, and fireballs. What else could he expect from Drago?

The vile king shot his black energy rays straight at Enzo, leaving the villager with no chance of escape. The true dark force had arrived in the music room.

Struggling to stay on his feet, Enzo gathered all that remained of his strength to grip the shield firmly. The dark light diverted to both sides of his body. It was obvious that Drago would kill him at any moment.

Drago was not going to give up.

Enzo was getting weaker by the second. His arms were losing strength. Finally, the hot shield flew out of his hands. Another stream of the nefarious rays was coming straight at him.

In an act of love, Martina threw herself before the beam of black energy. *"Sto-o-o-p!"* cried Martina. The dangerous power blasted the princess directly in her chest. Her body writhed in deep pain from the electric shock. She felt as if a thousand volts had reached her guts. The princess gasped and fell to the floor. Martina had sacrificed herself to save Enzo.

The flying shield hit a wall and bounced back, in time to divert the remaining evil rays back to its owner. The dark light reached Drago in his lazy eye. A loud roar of agony! His malevolent grin transformed to deep pain. The evil king lay face down on the ground and soon fell into a swoon. His ghostly appearance vanished slowly but completely.

"Nooooo!" sobbed Enzo, falling to his knees right next to Martina. Everything happened so fast he thought he still had the shield in his hand. "I can't lose you too!" He rested his head on Martina's burned dress.

There was an agonizing moment of total silence in the room.

"Please wake up!" sobbed Enzo. Tears spilled from his brown eyes and rolled down his cheeks.

Sore and disoriented, Martina could hear Enzo's voice, but her eyes were too heavy to open. She could not move a muscle. All her organs ached. It seemed as though someone were squeezing them as hard as he could. Unexpectedly, the strong pain transformed into a cold sensation. The princess felt the electricity traveling along all the veins in her body. She remained still, but her eyes suddenly projected a powerful beam of violet light that converted the ceiling hanging lamp into a beautiful large chandelier, all made of sand.

The strong force launched Enzo backward, crashing into a wall. His silhouette got stamped, leaving a perfect decorative outline on the wall. He ended up on the floor with a loud bang. Then, he hit his head against a doorknob; the last bump he was not expecting.

"Are you all right?" Martina followed every blow of her friend. It had to hurt.

"If that's what it takes for you to recover your powers, I'm perfectly fine!" Enzo smiled and rubbed the bump on his head at the same time.

"My magic is back!" Martina said. Her face lit up with enormous glee. Her eyes glowed glinting violet light. Her chest was still sore, but her happiness was stronger than the pain. Her love sacrifice had returned her magical powers.

There was finally a brief period of calm and even a little sparkle of romance.

"You sacrificed yourself for me?" asked Enzo in astonishment. At last, he realized everything that had happened.

"Yes!" Martina simply replied with a shy smile. A pink blush crept up her cheek.

In the sweet and perfect encounter, their eyes met. They held their tender gaze for a moment. But it could not last too long. Martina needed to act fast before Drago woke up.

"We must leave for Amo Island now!" said Martina, trying to hide her embarrassment.

"Of course!" responded Enzo, lifting the princess back to her feet.

The princess took one last look at her brother, a very sad one. Then her magic shimmered in the kingdom. Martina conjured up a sandstorm!

CHAPTER TWENTY-THREE

The powerful storm let its fury out. Strong gusts of sand invaded the farmlands and traveled toward the village. Trees were knocked down, and branches banged the tall walls of St. Cesca Cathedral. They blew away like arrows in a battle-field. The sand swirled around every corner of Enna Valley. It intensified by the minute. More sand arrived at the village. On Main Street, a huge cloud of sand began to spin faster rolling like a cylinder until a massive tornado was fully formed. The rumbling and buzzing sound of the wind was like a loud train crashing through the town.

The destination was clear. The whirling vortex shifted direction toward Diamond Palace. As it moved along Piano Plaza, the twister uprooted trees, sucking them into its powerful wind bands. Benches were ripped off at the foot of the deadly storm. The chunks of stones were pulverized more easily than a handful of wheat crackers. The unstoppable tornado finally reached the only building at the hilltop, Diamond Palace. The towers could not stand the strong gusts of wind. Glass shattered in all directions becoming flying lethal blades. The violent column of sand blasted away the windows of the music room.

The whole building shook hard.

King Drago, who had just regained consciousness, had a chance to open his eyes only to see the massive gust of sand coming straight at him. He was smashed against a wall. Fragments of plaster fell on top of the king. He was knocked unconscious on the floor, a second time. His body was covered with sand. The twister has done its job. After a couple of minutes, it started to dissolve. The hissing sound turned to mute. The room, which had been converted into a small desert, returned to its original condition.

A thick layer of sand hung over the entire valley. The wind began to subside, and the rain ceased. Calm returned to Enna Valley, and the flames were extinguished at Lusha Land.

At around midnight, the layer of sand had vanished entirely, and a violet full moon appeared, bringing light back to the kingdom. The sand had magically returned every structure to its place. All streets, houses, and even Piano Plaza recovered their vitality. Only brooms were needed to finish the cleanup. The village was about to get back the yearned-for look of its good days.

Mercy, who knew the princess very well, was certainly convinced that Martina's powers had arrived in Brightalia. With unshed tears in her eyes, Mercy was glad to see that the princess never abandoned her people. At dawn, Mercy got up very early, before the rest of the servants. She decided to check the palace to ensure everything was in order. She walked the business side of the palace first. Then, she entered the music room. Her head plunged to her hands when she found Drago lying on the floor.

Once her shock wore off, Mercy rushed to the king. He was still breathing. Only a few grains of sand remained on Drago's head.

Mercy screamed for help. Dante and Giorgina hurried to the music room.

"Please bring some water," instructed Mercy. The nanny loosened the collar of Drago's robe to make him more comfortable.

Dante went to fetch water, and Giorgina opened up the windows to fan the king with fresh air.

King Drago rested for at least thirty minutes more. He had failed to regain consciousness this time. He was in a perpetual fainting state.

The glass of water remained untouched. The king remained still. But Mercy decided not to wait any longer. She had a plan. She knew Drago needed some help. "I'll stay here until the king is stable. You can go back to the servants' quarters," Mercy told Dante and Giorgina.

Once they were gone, Mercy crept downstairs to the kitchens without making any noise. Donato was stirring a big pot of oatmeal.

"I hope I remember how to make the sleeping spell," whispered Mercy, biting her nails. The nanny tapped on Donato's shoulder.

The wooden spoon jumped to the air. Donato let out a scream. "You scared me to death!" said the cook, trying to catch some air.

"Sorry! I didn't mean to scare you," snickered Mercy. Then she got close to Donato's ear. "I need to put all the servants into a deep sleep," Mercy muttered. "I must take the king to Amo Island."

Donato's eyes widened. "Are you kidnapping King Drago?"

"No, I'm helping him." Mercy was convinced Martina could save Drago. "This delicious oatmeal you're preparing will carry a spell," whispered Mercy.

"I hope you know what you're doing." Donato scratched his sweaty chef hat.

"Don't worry. Everything will be fine," Mercy responded. She did not want to take any risks. She knew it was tough to convince all the servants to allow her to take the king to his sister. The spell was the perfect solution to execute her plan quickly.

The nanny was ready to start. She thought for a moment. Then she added some herbs to the pot. One was still alive and coiled around her arm. "Get inside!" ordered Mercy, untangling the climbing plant and sticking it inside the large cauldron. Then she pronounced the magical words, with a single wand flourish. *Ancora Siestare Jinxa!*

Bright yellow rays shot from the ivory wand straight at the pot. The oatmeal bubbled over onto the stove. Mercy and Donato jumped back. After a minute or two, the bubbles turned into a light smoke that vanished in the air, leaving the kitchen with a pleasant smell.

"It looks … almost perfect!" admitted Mercy. She hoped she remembered the spell correctly. It had been many years since she decided to leave the wizardry school.

Mercy straightened her apron and looked at Donato. "You're so happy that the storm is gone, that you will serve the oatmeal to everybody for breakfast." Mercy winked at the cook.

"I can handle that task," responded Donato, winking back at the nanny.

Back at the music room, King Drago remained unconscious. Mercy moved the king slowly to a couch. The devoted nanny patiently sat beside Drago and waited.

It did not take too long for Donato to show up at the room. He stopped at the open doorway. His eyes were as big as two tennis balls.

"What's wrong?" asked Mercy. She wondered if the spell had

not worked properly for the servants.

"I dished out the oatmeal to everybody, and they're all sleeping like babies," said the cook. "I didn't expect the spell to act so fast!"

"That's actually great!" answered Mercy, feeling some relief. She stood ready to implement her risky plan. "Let's move on then."

Donato hesitated. "Are you sure you want to seize the king?" he asked. The cook stared at Drago. Even in his sleep, the king looked arrogant. Donato was still not too convinced about Mercy's idea.

"Please, Donato! Martina is the only one who can save him. If she sent the sand storm, she must know how to end the perpetual sleep," explained Mercy. "We don't have time to lose."

Donato lifted the king's arm, and it fell back down like a puppet. Drago was completely asleep. "Okay. Let's do it!" Donato finally agreed, removing his chef's hat.

"Thank you! We must take Drago to the royal carriage," explained Mercy.

They helped each other to carry the king to the back yard. Near the passageway that led to the stables was the carriage.

"What are you doing?" asked the stable boy. His eyes jumped when he saw the two servants carrying the king. "Is King Drago dead?

Mercy and Donato froze in place. They rested the king on the ground. Donato had completely forgotten about the stable boy. Mercy was trying to come up with an explanation.

But Donato was quicker than her. Before the guy could say another word, the cook knocked him down with a single punch. "Problem solved!" Donato shook his sore hand. His knuckles were red, but his face showed a proud look.

"Wow! I did not know the strong side of you!" smiled Mercy.

"I also have my hidden talents," teased Donato, showing his fat and flabby biceps. He went ahead and tried to lay the king down on the seat of the carriage. "There is not enough space. We better sit him down."

"Be careful! Hold his head," requested Mercy. She was helping from the other side of the coach.

"I'm trying," responded Donato, letting out a long sigh of tiredness.

Mercy rushed to the storerooms and soon returned with a navy blanket to cover Drago. "Ouch!" The nanny bumped her head on the carriage's door. "Why am I doing all this?"

"Good question." Donato turned to the nanny.

Mercy's eyes clouded with tears. "It has been many years that I have served the royal family." After a few more minutes of struggle, Mercy was ready to leave Diamond Palace.

Donato opened the side gates. "Good luck!" he said, waving at Mercy. Right away, the two horses started galloping toward the beach.

Mercy made it to Amo Island without a hitch. It had been a long morning, and it was not over yet. The cunning nanny stopped the carriage in front of Martina's small house. She patted the horses for the nice ride and went inside.

"Mercy! It's so nice to see you again," said Martina, hugging her loyal nanny. "You have no idea of the horrible things that have happened."

"I can only imagine." Mercy wrapped her arms around the princess. She looked at the kitchen. All the cookware was made of sand. Then she turned her gaze back to the princess, and grabbing her hands, she added, "The storm returned life to the valley and ended the devastating fires at the farmlands, but—" The dryness in her throat made her pause a second long. "It did not help Drago."

"What do you mean?" A puzzled frown appeared on Martina's face. She went on to provide an explanation. "I gave my brother a blow of magic. I'll destroy the red book, and then he will forget all about his dark powers."

"Well, the blow of magic went a little bit too far. Drago is in a perpetual fainting state. He has not recovered his consciousness yet," said Mercy with a concerned look. "You must help your brother."

Martina recalled everything that she had lived through the previous night – how Drago had transformed into an evil monster and had been determined to kill her and Enzo. The princess said firmly, "No, I must find and destroy the Sagerant first. This is actually perfect."

Mercy walked close to Martina. "That might be too late to revive him. His heart can stop any minute," insisted the nanny.

Some of the orphan children came out of a room wondering what was going on.

Martina walked her fingers over the kitchen counter. After some hesitation, she stated again, "I can't help him right now!" The princess had always loved her family unconditionally, but Drago had become blind to his arbitrary ruling. To the extreme, he was willing to kill for power. It was sad and also frustrating for the princess. She had struggled, against her brother's will, to help her kingdom and make things right.

"Martina! Don't forget your family values, what you learned from your parents." Mercy's voice was soft and kind. She opened a cupboard, picked up a jar, and served herself a glass of water. Then she poured the rest of the water into a big bowl and gave it to the princess. "Do you remember all the love King Alessio and Queen Costanza gave you? Everything they did to protect you, to help your brother recover from the horse accident? They were always there for you. Please don't abandon Drago now."

Martina's heart wrinkled like a prune. She found herself twirling Mercy's words in her mind. She knew she loved her brother. She remembered when they were little kids and played together. Martina looked at the bowl of water and saw her reflection, the good Martina she had always known. It was then that the princess realized she had to get her brother out of his perpetual sleep. "Where is Drago?"

Clapping her hands, Mercy walked toward the entrance of the house and pushed the front door open. Her face showed a wide toothy grin.

"It's Drago?" Martina shot her head inside the royal carriage.

"Yes! I had to put all the servants under a spell," explained Mercy in a proud posture.

"How did you do that?" asked Martina, smiling.

"Ahhh! I have my secrets too." Mercy smiled back at Martina. "I went to a wizardry school for a couple of years, but it wasn't really what I like. My vocation was to be a nanny! Dante helped me to fake my magic background check so that I could work with the royal family."

"You both kept a good secret!" Martina turned her gaze to her brother, and then back to Mercy. "Let's take Drago to my room."

"Hello, hello!" Enzo showed up at the house. He glanced at the carriage, but he did not notice the king.

"Long time without seeing you," Mercy told Enzo.

"I know," he said. "Don't I look more handsome and—"

"Mercy came here to bring Drago." Martina interrupted the nice talk. "He's in a perpetual fainting state, and I have to save him." The princess opened the door of the carriage. "I'm glad you are here. You can give us a hand to take him inside."

"Holy magnolia! Are you out of your mind? Your brother was about to kill both of us last night," grumbled Enzo. He walked away from the carriage. "Now, I have to carry the dead dragon?"

He paced in circles and added, "Don't count on me."

"Drago is *not dead!*" said Martina. "He's just in a deep sleep." The princess gave Enzo a one-minute version of what had happened to Drago, treading right behind him.

Enzo kicked some sand toward the carriage. He did not believe what he was about to answer. He sighed and then said, "Let's do it then." He stared at Drago, shaking his head. "All I have to do for Brightalia ... carrying a numb king!"

Still listening to Enzo's endless complaints, they took Drago to Martina's small, but comfy bed. The princess prepared a special potion that carried her magic and gave it to her brother every hour.

It was getting late, and King Drago remained unconscious. They all hoped he would wake up in the morning.

CHAPTER TWENTY-FOUR

I t was almost dawn, and the sun was starting to show its rays.
Martina's bright violet eyes were wide open. It had been just a quick fitful sleep for the princess. She had tossed from side to side all night. The princess kept thinking about her brother.

Martina looked at her diary. It showed a green color, but there was not a magical word on the cover. *What does the color green mean?* Martina was very anxious. She bit the corner of her lip. So many things had happened lately, she did not know what to believe anymore! It was one of the moments she missed her parents the most. *If only they were here. If only I could get their advice!*

Mercy continued to rest in the room as well as all the kids, and Enzo still sank on a sofa like a mummy.

Martina could not wait a minute longer. She went to check on Drago. He slept like a newborn baby. *What will be his reaction when he awakes?* Martina wasn't sure. She should expect the worse. Just to be safe, she decided to tie her brother's legs to the bed.

"Let me exercise some caution here," said Martina, pulling hard on a knot.

Martina stood at the door waiting for the uncertain moment. She was getting impatient. She softly hit her head against the doorframe, once. And twice. And several times. It was stressful until finally, King Drago opened his eyes.

Martina remained at the door. Calm returned to her. She quietly observed her brother who had not noticed her presence.

Drago's blue eyes appeared to have changed color to a light violet.

Martina was surprised to see the color change. *Does that mean that Drago also got some of my special powers?*

Right in front of Drago, there was a dresser. On the mirror, a handwritten note said, "You are my brother, and I will always love you."

With his still blurry vision, Drago could read the note. He instantly realized he was not at Diamond Palace.

At the edge of the dresser was Martina's wooden box. A tall window next to the magical box allowed Drago to view the island. Martina's face was engraved in every direction the king could move his eyes. Drago felt a whirlwind of emotions inside of him. A river of water filled his eyes.

Martina walked closer to her brother.

Lying on the bed, Drago turned his head toward Martina. "I cannot! I cannot change!" wailed Drago. He tried to move his legs.

"Yes, you can! Look deep inside your heart," cried Martina.

"Untie my legs!" The king was enraged to find himself bound to the bed. He pulled hard on one of the ropes. He was very upset.

"Calm down, please!" implored Martina. "Close your eyes and feel your good heart pumping," Martina said softly.

Drago breathed deeply. He remained still. "You're right," he finally admitted.

Martina started to remove the ropes from Drago's legs. "Changing takes courage, but it's worth it."

Drago did not move or pronounce a word. But it had all been an act. As soon as Martina finished removing the last rope, the king lunged at her. "Who do you think you are to do this to me?"

"Please, let me explain." Martina tussled with Drago until she managed to escape from his arms. She raced across the house. In a flash, she wondered if she had taken the right step. Drago did not seem to be cooperating. The princess opened the front door, and tripping over some loose rocks, she hit the sand.

Enzo jumped from the sofa with a scream when he saw Drago chasing Martina.

"Stay on your beach and leave me alone!" Drago slammed the door almost breaking it.

"For once in your life... If you could listen to me," sobbed Martina. She got up, limping. She could tell her brother was still blind to the chaos he had created in Brightalia. He did not understand that true power was based on respect, trust, and love for others. For Martina, that was the legitimate way to control people, not fear. The princess had no idea how to make Drago change his mind. Unexpectedly, she saw a brown shirt ahead of her.

Enzo had raced past Drago and stood before Martina.

"Move out of the way, cheap peasant!" Drago said bitterly. He walked a couple of steps forward, but the kids also dashed from inside the house and stood beside Enzo.

"If you touch Martina, I'll fight you," added one of the young boys, waving his fists at Drago.

Mercy also rushed out holding a sword.

Then the neighbors, one by one, came from their houses and lined up before the children, Enzo, and Mercy. It did not take long for most of the sand village to step forward to protect Martina from her brother. Some even carried sticks, rakes, and staves ready to battle the king.

"Back off!" yelled Drago with haughty eyes and a proud heart. Nobody moved.

Drago grinned conceitedly. His monumental arrogance still seethed in him. "I can have every single house here burned to the ground and all your heads chopped off! He threw a burning hard stare at the crowd. His eyes were rigid and cold. Then he asked, "Will you still defend my sister?

Mercy scrambled to the front in a couple of strides. She handed Drago the sword and said fearlessly, "Kill me now, for I will fight for Martina to my last breath, even against the King of Brightalia!"

"We're ready to die for your sister." This came from one of the farmers who stepped ahead of the group. He sank his pole hard in the sand. The rest of the peasants pointed their homemade weapons at the king.

Master Fabrizio stood at a distance, observing the crowd.

Drago's jaw dropped in total disbelief. Nobody stood behind the king, the true and only ruler of Brightalia. King Drago was alone! He had never felt so outcast and forsaken before. His stern look wanted to convert into sadness, but he managed to hide his feelings. The imperious king dropped the sword, jumped on a horse, and rode off.

"Please wait!" wept Martina, extending her arms.

For long days and nights, everybody at the sand village waited for the royal army to arrive and kill them all. The new farms were going to be burned down to ashes. But the villagers were ready to fight for Martina. They felt immensely proud of the girl, who against all kingdom regulations, managed to channel her energy and magical powers to benefit them, the workers of Brightalia.

Just a week later, what they anticipated happened. The king's messenger came to Amo Island. He rode in a chariot, a two-wheeled carriage drawn by horses. A long line of escorting knights followed close behind him on their horses. They looked like a living fortress. Navy surcoats, with brown belts around their waists, were placed over their heavy body armors. The surcoats were emblazoned with the Brightalia coat of arms. One of the knights carried the official flag of the kingdom. The rest were well accompanied by all sorts of weapons including swords, crossbows, battle axes, and lances.

The peasants arrived like droves of cattle. Martina, Enzo, and Mercy also stood at the Sand Plaza, waiting for the bad news or the first arrow.

Standing in the golden chariot, General Althar unrolled a scroll and announced:

To all the nobles and farmers of this village,
Due to the unforeseen disappearance of King Drago,
We, the Royal Army and the Council of Brightalia,
Under an emergency decree,
Have unanimously declared that ...

Althar looked at Martina and fixed his velvet cap in place. Then he continued with his proclamation:

Princess Martina shall take the Brightalia throne.

Martina stared at Althar as if an alien had just landed in front of her. Her heart was beating so strong she thought her chest would burst.

The General went on to conclude his short speech:

To all to whom this announcement comes,
Shall be informed, this declaration is official and effective as of today,
In the land of the sand, from coast to coast,
On the 520th day of the White Whale Year.

"But I am not—" Martina tried to respond.

"You're the true Queen of Brightalia." Althar kindly interrupted. "I will support you in everything you need."

"Me?" asked Martina with watery eyes. She never expected those words. It was true that she had helped many people, and that they had shown their loyalty to her, but to be the queen? She looked at the crowd. It was hard to believe that Drago had abandoned the throne, his power, and control! A rush of questions whirled in the princess's mind. *Is it my time to fill my dad's shoes?* The girl who was born on Eagle Sunday... The girl who had to conceal her powers because her mom was afraid of magic... But the girl who still used her magic to give roofs and food to so many needy families. Maybe it's the time to prove that the same girl can also rule a kingdom. Martina stepped forward from the multitude and making a curtsy, she responded, "It will be my grateful honor."

The entire village burst into applause and happy cheers.

Enzo bowed to the future queen. Mercy hugged Martina with great affection.

Althar leapt off the chariot and approached the princess. "The Royal Council will make the necessary arrangements for your coronation," gushed the Chief of Army with a satisfied grin on his face. "It shall be a special day for our kingdom. We trust Brightalia will be in excellent hands."

"Thank you, Althar," responded Martina. She was still trying to absorb the royal proclamation and the news about her brother. "Is it true? Where is Drago?" she asked with concern.

"King Drago is missing. Nobody knows where he is or if he will ever return to Diamond Palace." Those were the final words of the king's messenger as he climbed back in his chariot and led his line of knights out of the sand village.

CHAPTER TWENTY-FIVE

On the morning of Martina's coronation, everybody at Diamond Palace was very busy making all the preparations. A happy mood had returned to the royal residence. The princess was going to be the youngest queen to hold the Brightalia throne, but maybe the most popular one.

The ceremony was going to be unlike any seen before, cheerful but simple. Just like Martina! There were no formal invitations sent out, and there was no dress code to observe. The doors of the main balcony were going to be opened for all Brightalians at Piano Plaza to enjoy the coronation of the new queen. For the first time, the village could witness the entire ceremony. Everybody was thrilled. Villagers were sewing, ironing, and picking out their best attire for the celebration.

Martina decorated her own gold dress. The center of the gown was ornamented with colorful sand gems. The slightly puffy sleeves and lace in the back added to the overall beauty of the piece. The modest, but nice dress was ready for the future queen.

The grand ballroom shone in white and gold. All flower arrangements were enchanting with lilies and iris, all made of sand. The celebration feast was not the typical one. It was going to be served in a tent in the middle of Piano Plaza. It was very important for Martina to feed all her people, especially the poor.

At sundown, Diamond Palace glowed in white, gold, and violet. It looked impressive as the colors created a beam of light shining all the way up to the sky.

Piano Plaza was getting packed with people. They were all eager to witness the coronation of the fiftieth ruler of the Kingdom of Brightalia, traditionally called the Golden King or the Golden Queen in this case.

Sharp at seven o'clock, St. Cesca Cathedral's bells pealed fifty times. After the last ring, trumpets announced the start of the ceremony at Diamond Palace.

The guards opened the double doors that led to the main staircase descending to the grand ballroom. There stood Martina, for the last time as a princess. Her lovely gown swayed from side to side as she walked down the stairs. A simple violet cloak enhanced her silhouette.

The bishop gave Martina a joyful look. He rose and started his prayer. "Bless Lord, this queen…"

The audience also stood. The crowd at the plaza kept silent.

Martina respectfully took the coronation oath. She made her solemn promise to govern Brightalia according to the kingdom's laws and customs and to maintain the welfare and peace of Brightalia, its people, and its lands.

The bishop turned the page of the Sovereignty Book of State.

The Coronation Act was amended, and now Martina needed to take an additional oath. "Will you protect, defend, and rule for the good of Brightalia and all its acquired lands, being

Lusha Land or any new territory procured during the length of your reign?" declared the bishop.

"I will," responded Martina who continued with her right hand raised until she made that last oath.

Martina wanted to follow the family tradition. With great respect, she decided to wear Queen Constanza's crown. The awaited moment finally came. But when everybody looked at the stand, the crown was missing.

"The queen's crown has been stolen," a servant said.

A hush fell over the royal guests. At Piano Plaza, heads shook in disbelief.

Martina placed her hands on her chest. Her heart pounded hard.

At the far end of the grand ballroom, a secret door opened. All eyes flicked to the door. A tall man moved slowly into the room. It was Drago! He held the crown. The unexpected silence amplified at the ballroom and Piano Plaza.

Drago was simply wearing a plain white shirt and navy loose pants. He walked toward Martina. He bowed to his sister and placed the crown on Martina's head. Then, he whispered softly in Martina's ear, "You are my sister, and I will always love you."

Those were the most gratifying and fulfilling words that Martina could have ever heard from her brother. She knew her brother had changed. She was so content and relieved. Martina held the crown with one hand and curtsied to Drago. A cute dimple appeared below her sparkling eyes. Her heart returned to normal beating.

The bishop hurried next to Martina and in a solemn voice intoned, "Receive this Orb and remember that the Kingdom of Brightalia is subject to the Power of Light. As a monarch of this

Land, you shall only reign under the light side of the Force."

Martina extended her left hand to receive the orb. Drago handed the scepter to the bishop.

The senior priest proceeded with the ceremony. He looked at the Sovereignty Book of State again, and read, "Receive this Royal Scepter, the Symbol of Power, Justice, and Equity." He closed the State book. His face held a smile. He edged next to the queen, and proclaimed, "On the nineteenth hour of this day, I name you Martina II, ruler of the Kingdom of Brightalia."

Martina was named after her maternal triple great-grandmother or great, great, great grandmother. She decided to keep her name in honor of Martina I of Brightalia.

Drago held Martina's hand tightly and then raised it. "Lords and Ladies, I present to you the Golden Queen of Brightalia, Her Majesty, Martina II!" Drago glanced at the crowd, feeling proud of his sister.

The silence broke and everybody cheered for the new queen. Piano Plaza went wild. "Queen Martina, Queen Martina…"

Martina was immersed in happiness. Her heart fluttered as the wings of a butterfly.

"You deserve all the ovation and acclaim!" whispered Drago. He listened to the multitude. You're the true hero and Queen of Brightalia."

With her enchanting smile, Queen Martina proceeded to sit on the throne.

Drago assisted the queen. He fixed Martina's gown. "I'll take care of Your Majesty." Two servants observed as Drago did their job. He was thoughtful and compassionate. The look on his face revealed his healing heart.

"Thank you for coming," said Martina.

"I could not miss this historical event," responded Drago. Then he pulled out of his pocket a violet diamond necklace.

Delicately putting it on Martina's neck, Drago added, "I hope this precious stone will remind you that I will always be thankful for all the love you have given me."

"In my heart, it will always be," responded Martina, looking straight into Drago's eyes.

They hugged each other. Martina did not expect to receive the crown from her brother. It was a great pleasure for the new queen.

Drago stayed for a quick dance with his sister, but soon after that, he left Diamond Palace.

Queen Martina went out to the main balcony. She was impressed! There were people everywhere. People climbed on statues and columns and hung out of trees. She felt so loved and welcomed. She waved at all her people, just as she did when she was a young girl.

Instead of ending with an exhibition of fireworks, Martina requested the release of sky lanterns in memory of those who had passed away in the Lusha Land battles. The hot balloons freely floated in the air. The night was fresh and a sentiment of peace was felt in every heart.

"I will keep dreaming for Brightalia," murmured Martina. Her eyes blurred. She glanced up at the sky wondering if her parents would feel proud of her. Just then, a star shot across the sky. With a winning smile on her face, she answered back, blowing out a kiss into the air.

Later, inside the main ballroom, Martina found Enzo blushing in the corner. She could see he felt very out of place amidst all the grandeur. It was the first time that the peasant did not watch a kingdom event from Piano Plaza. Queen Martina moved near her good friend.

"It's so nice to have you here," said the queen with affection.

Enzo could not avoid stealing a brief glance at the queen's gown. "You look … you look … spectacular!" The peasant finally finished, overcoming his stutter.

"Oh! I added my magical touch," explained Martina, looking down at the gems on her dress. The new queen wanted to enjoy her special night, her moment of happiness. "The music is so nice!" she added in a soft voice, peering at the dance floor.

With great respect and a pinch of shyness, the humble villager went ahead and extended one arm. "Could we dance?" asked Enzo, putting the other arm behind his back, like a true royal gentleman.

Martina bobbed a friendly curtsy to Enzo. "With the King of the Sea, the only answer is yes!" The queen raised her arm until her satin glove reached Enzo's hand.

Enzo softly clasped the queen's hand and allowed his other hand to reach her back. They swayed slowly from side to side. Then they twirled with ease around the dance floor until they found themselves spinning. They felt so comfortable after overcoming their shyness that they even did some beautiful pirouettes. The long flowing dress of the queen waved in perfect time to the music.

Many happy eyes drifted to the cute couple. One by one, guests gathered around them in delight.

Martina's heart also whirled inside her chest, and her feet seemed to have lost contact with the ground. She thought she was floating. She felt she was in a dream.

They smiled at each other, and finally the special moment came. Enzo gave Martina a quick, but romantic kiss. One that was more than perfect for the queen. Just as she had fantasized about it!

CHAPTER TWENTY-SIX

The next morning, Queen Martina was ready to start her new job. She was the first one to enter the Council's hall. She sat on the royal chair even though she felt kind of uncomfortable. She looked super small between the armrests of the gold and blue velvet chair.

All the members arrived on time, including Lord Porto and the other councilors who had been locked up in the dungeons. Lord Abewell also attended the assembly. Queen Martina herself requested his return.

The queen's goal was clear – to rebuild her kingdom. She wanted everything to be given back to her people, especially their farms. She proposed the elimination of all the unfair reforms that Drago had imposed on the citizens. At the end of her initial address, Queen Martina said, "And this is all for our people. Brightalians deserve no less than a prosperous kingdom. A kingdom of happiness. A kingdom of peace…" the queen raised her gaze.

The entire audience paid close attention to the speech.

"Brightalia will rise and shine again!" finished Martina.

A clap was heard. Then another one. Then appreciative

applause became louder and warmer. The whole Council stood.

Martina observed the cheerful faces. She was pleased the committee approved and supported her new initiatives. She gave a slight bob of her head, signaling the culmination of the session.

But before Queen Martina left, she motioned Lord Campo to come to the front of the room.

"Yes, Your Majesty," said the emissary, walking at a brisk pace.

"I have a special assignment for you. A very important one."

"Go ahead, Your Majesty," responded Lord Campo eager to hear what the queen would propose. "How can I be of help?"

"I want you to go to Castella as our messenger for peace." Martina rested her hands on the royal chair. She knew the Lusha Land conflict was very complicated. She also understood that cultivating the fields was the life of many farmers. Martina craved to return ranchers their freedom to be the creators of the most delicious agricultural products. The farming problem although significantly reduced with the new crops at Amo Island, still remained a concern for the kingdom. "We don't want any more battles. We don't need to lose any more lives. We want to go back to negotiate an agreement to fairly distribute the claimed land between the two kingdoms."

The emissary mused on the queen's petition. It was a tough one. But Lord Campo always worked very closely with King Alessio on this problem. He was the best candidate to act as a peacemaker. He knew it and ultimately agreed, "I will do my best, Your Majesty. I'll leave for Castella early in the morning." Lord Campo raised his glasses as though he could see well without them. Or maybe he wished his blurred vision could reveal a new insight of how to be a successful mediator.

"I hope we're lucky for once and for all!" said Queen Martina.

Martina also wanted to renew the Market. It was sad to see it as a distribution center. For that task, Martina counted on Enzo. The nice fish salesman gathered a group of friends and put them to work. They built new carts, replaced the rusty doors, fixed the leaking ceiling, and repaired the cracks in the stone walls.

"We are pleased to reopen the doors of 'Dream Market,'" said Queen Martina at the inauguration ceremony.

Enzo stood beside the queen and saluted the mass of people gathered outside the mart.

"This is your home, the heart and product of our lands. Make it shine!" The queen got ready to cut the violet ribbon. But then she turned to Enzo. "You worked hard for the market. Cut the ribbon."

"No, no, no … you cut the ribbon." Enzo gave Queen Martina an embarrassed look.

"I want you to cut the ribbon," insisted the Queen.

The crowd stared at the queen and the fisher.

"It's a royal order!" whispered Queen Martina, handing the scissors to Enzo. She crossed her arms and smiled at Enzo.

Enzo smiled back. He got a tight grip on the scissors and cut the violet ribbon. "Welcome to Dream Market!"

People cheered from the street. The guards opened the heavy doors of the marketplace. The remodeling made the place look brand new.

"I want to show you something." Martina pulled Enzo by the hand.

"What is it?" Enzo asked with a chortle.

Queen Martina headed toward the area where Enzo had his old stand.

"This spot looks familiar," joked Enzo.

Queen Martina opened the rear door of the Market.

Enzo froze in place. His jaw dropped and his brown eyes got round.

Martina wanted her good friend to finally turn a dream into a reality. The queen had bought Enzo a special gift.

"Wo ... wo ... wow! A fishing boat for me?" Enzo could barely speak. "Buuut, I can't accept this."

"There are no returns, no exchanges, or refunds," Martina told Enzo with a wink.

Enzo had no choice but to laugh.

"Make your King of the Sea story a reality," wished Queen Martina. She saw how Enzo was still paralyzed in place. "Hey! You're free to move now."

"Thank you ... *thank you!*" Enzo hugged Martina. Or in better words, he squeezed Martina until she could hardly breathe. Then he pecked her on the lips.

"You like it?" asked Martina, catching some air.

"No, I don't like it! Enzo frowned and folded his arms. "I love it!" He then screamed with happiness.

They sat on the boat and after chatting and steering the helm for a little while, Queen Martina asked, "Can you meet me at Diamond Palace right at midnight?" Her look was serious now, but Enzo was too excited to notice.

"Is it New Year yet?" joked Enzo.

"This is serious!" Martina said.

"As you command, Your Majesty," said Enzo with a military salute.

Enzo arrived at Diamond Palace on the dot, not a minute before or late. Once there, he realized he never asked Martina what they were going to do. Maybe he was getting another special surprise. A midnight buffet with fountains of chocolate and a rain of goblin candy!

For years, the humble fisher had yearned to try the sweet treat from Troll Bakery. To his bad luck, chocolate was only sold to nobles due to its limited quantities. At least, that was what Mama Troll claimed.

While his mouth watered, the villager got ready to strike one of the giant door knockers. "Tonight will be great. I can feel it," muttered Enzo as he finally swung the metal ring of the lion head knocker.

"Hi!" Queen Martina opened the front doors herself. All servants were already sleeping. She noticed Enzo was well dressed. "You look …" A quick pause. "Classy," admitted the queen. But she was not particularly planning a ball.

Enzo checked out some family portraits in the foyer. Then he traced his fingers along a thick book. It was the original Brightalia history book, only kept at Diamond Palace.

Martina opened up the heavy book to the first page. "You know … I want to change our history," Martina said quickly. She flipped the page. Martina was happy Drago had redeemed himself, but she still wanted to destroy the wizardry book to prevent any future ruler from getting a hold of the cryptic book, or even worse, using black magic. "I must find the Sagerant and burn it."

"Great! That red book only brings trouble," responded Enzo. He continued to look around. His white shirt and khaki baggy pants were almost perfectly pressed. "But why am I here?"

Martina coughed slightly and said, "To help me search for the dark book of magic!"

"*What?*" asked Enzo, quite disappointed. "I can't believe that's why you asked me to come. I always have to be at the edge of danger." He blew away the hair from his forehead.

"Please! It's very important for me," said the queen with a pleading look in her eyes. She needed to ensure her brother's dark magic memory was completely erased. "My best guess is that it must be in the library or in Drago's room.

"Why me? Why me?" Enzo paced around and around. He looked at Martina. "You have to double twist my ankle for that."

The queen showed her white teeth at Enzo. "*Puhlease!*"

Enzo could not refuse. Sighing, he said, "Okay … okay, one more time!"

"I knew you would help me!" Martina climbed up the stairs.

Enzo mounted the steps right behind the queen. "I don't have nice memories of this place," murmured the fisher as he made it to the second floor.

Martina stopped in the middle of the main corridor. "You can check Drago's room, and I'll take the library."

"No way! This one is not flying!" Enzo kept walking toward the library. "I won't go to the Dragon's room."

"But the library is much bigger."

"I can handle big!" called Enzo almost at the door of the library room.

Enzo searched every corner of the room. He hunted through every shelf, even the ones on top, close to the ceiling. The rolling ladder got stuck a couple of times, but he finished every row of books. He looked inside drawers and dusty wooden trunks. He checked the head, body, and legs of every piece of armor. He was convinced the red book was not there.

"What time is it?" asked Martina, entering the Library. She read her diary.

Enzo came down from the creaky wood ladder. "It's a quarter

past not happening," he answered. "The Sagerant is not here. Where could your wily brother have hidden it?"

Martina plopped down on a couch. She did not seem to listen. The queen was engrossed in the words of her journal. "A math problem," she said in a whisper.

Enzo cast a quick look over the queen's shoulder. "What is it?"

"I couldn't find the red book in Drago's room, but I found this. Look!" Martina pointed at the faint writing. "The diary is giving me a formula." Queen Martina went ahead and read it aloud:

This formula is a success,
But it can also be a mess.
Just go from East to West,
If you ever need to guess.

There are thirty-five on one side,
And thirty more to decide,
Find the prime number in between,
To sum to the golden kings.
The second root of me,
Must be added to the three.
Be patient. Don't get bored!
Finally take away number four.

If you got all the way down,
You made this formula count,
Now embrace and savor the race,
You're at the right place!

"Wait an atom!" A spark flared in Enzo's brain. "Maybe the diary is telling you where the red book is." He took a closer look at the puzzle.

"You think?"

"Yep, I got it!" Enzo raised his eyes off the book to meet Martina's. "The Sagerant is hidden in the columns of Piano Plaza." He jerked his fist down proud of his analysis.

"You're right. Sixty-five!" Martina snapped her fingers. "There are sixty-five columns at the plaza."

"Simple huh?" said Enzo. "But who is going to figure out the rest?" Math was not one of the villager's strong subjects.

"A formula about the columns in Piano Plaza." Martina read the page several times. Then she grabbed the pencil. "Just need a little bit of logic to solve it."

"Hah! You understand it?" Enzo scratched his head.

"Give me a minute! I'm sure I can do this."

Enzo saw how Martina scribbled some numbers. It definitely looked like a honors math problem to him, but still, he was able to puzzle out one more line. "Oh yeah! The golden kings represent the number fifty."

"Yeah!" said Martina. "And I have the answer: eight! It's column number eight."

"Is it really?"

"I might not know too much about spells because of my mom, but I do know my math."

At once, Martina and Enzo headed to Piano Plaza. On the way, they picked up some hammers, axes, and picks.

Martina used her violet eyes' rays to illuminate the marble columns. They were clustered with gods, saints, goblins, demons, and all types of weird imaginary creatures.

"My favorite demon is the Water Eeltune," teased Enzo. "He's the terror of the ocean."

"Hey! We had to fight a pretty bad monster, and it was not fun at all."

"That's why I say those creepy monsters should be erased

from all pillars!" Enzo imitated a gravelly voice. The villager was about to hit the base of the eighth West column. But he had to stop his blow in midway at the scream of Martina.

"Wait Enzo! We have to do this right." Martina turned to her diary and read the beginning of the formula again:

> This formula is a success,
> But it can also be a mess.
> Just go from East to West,
> If you ever need to guess.

"If we have to guess, we start counting from the East," clarified Martina.

They were standing at the wrong column.

"I knew it! It's the eighth column from the East! Enzo took the tools and followed Martina who got to the correct eighth pillar in a flash.

Martina observed all the fanciful sculpting. "I hope the wizardry book is here!"

"No more than me," replied Enzo, jumping into action. "Move to the side because this job is mine!" He started pounding the column with heavy beatings of his hammer. After various attempts, he was able to crack the layers of marble. The center of the column, made of wood, finally became exposed. A small part of the book was also visible. "Here is your Sagerant," said Enzo out of breath. His face shone like a freshly washed carriage, but of sweat.

Martina placed her hand on the column. It was pretty rough. Right then, the wood came alive. The trunk grew thicker, and climbing plants twined around Martina's hands in no time. "Let me go!" she screamed. But more vines wound around her. Pieces of marble flew in all directions, leaving exposed the black tree, which was already taller than any of the columns.

"Don't panic! I'll get you out of there." Enzo, in a single jump, picked up the ax and slammed it at the furious trailing plants, trying to break the slender stem grabbing the queen.

Yes! The vines were thin but very strong.

Enzo could see how creepers were cutting Martina's skin. "Leave her alone."

The trunk started taking some shape. It became a weird grotesque monster. It grew a white lazy eye that glanced in all directions.

Enzo immediately recalled the incident at the music room with Drago. "Hit the eye!" shouted Enzo, pulling hard on the evil stems.

Martina glared at the tree or monster. Or whatever it could be called. "You'll never use my brother again!" She projected her violet rays straight at the white eye. The wood instantly dissolved to sawdust. Much to her relief, the red book landed in her hand. Martina grasped it tightly. "I have it."

They had found the mysterious book that had been missing for so many years and that had caused so much suffering for the kingdom. They hugged each other, jumping around column number eight from the East!

The burning part was the easy one. They even got to roast some gnome-mallows over the fire. And Enzo finally ate chocolate for the first time.

Queen Martina had achieved most of her goals for Brightalia. The Red Sagerant was destroyed. The streets of the village regained their vitality. Gardens were in full bloom. Birds dressed the top of the trees, and the music was back at Enna Valley. Everything was going great until Lord Campo returned from Castella. The Lusha Land report was alarming!

CHAPTER TWENTY-SEVEN

Martina showed Enzo the portrait of King Alessio. It still hung on the wall of the Diamond Office.

"Wherever he is, he must be very proud of—" Enzo almost finished when Lord Campo appeared in a hurry at the door.

The Emissary to Land Resources dropped a bundle of papers on the table. His lips were trembling as if he were going to let out a sob. But he never cried. His face was as white as the snow. In fact, it looked like he was about to faint. But he stayed on his feet. His gaze was fixed on the roll of documents.

Martina flinched at the face of the emissary. She could not put a finger on his emotion. Worried? Depressed? Fatigued? Finally, she figured it out. All of them! "What happened?" Martina asked with trepidation.

Lord Campo drew in a breath of sharp air, but he did not have a chance to answer the queen's question.

"A huge army amassed on the border," explained General Althar in a panting voice. He had flown inside the room faster than an arrow. His hand was on his cap to keep it in place.

Martina turned her eyes to the general. "What huge army?"

General Althar flicked the dust off his uniform and added,

"Castella's, Your Majesty."

"King Filippo didn't accept any type of negotiation," Lord Campo finally managed to explain. He adjusted his thick glasses and showed Martina one of the documents. "He refused to sign our proposed agreement, and in revenge for what he described as a dare, he ordered his army to attack us again." The emissary looked down at the floor. Then he continued with a broken voice, "I cannot be more frustrated and disappointed with my failed attempt to end this conflict."

Martina stiffened at the news. Yet she understood it was not Campo's fault. "You don't have to blame yourself. Castella is a war-hungry kingdom, and King Filippo has always looked at Brightalia with greedy eyes." She stared at the unsigned agreement Lord Campo gave her.

"We can fight again. Brightalia will beat down Castella in one last and final battle!" said Enzo fiercely. "I'm ready to serve my kingdom!"

General Althar shook his head. "Our army has already been defeated. There is nothing we can do." Althar glanced up at the portrait of King Alessio. His eyes welled up with tears, something very unusual. "It appears we won't only lose Lusha Land, but Brightalia as well."

That was when Queen Martina choked. She felt as if her heart had sunk to the bottom of the deepest ocean. "That's not possible!" After all her effort, she was going to lose her kingdom. "We can't sit here with our arms crossed and do nothing."

"Your Majesty, we have no soldiers." General Althar said with a desperate look on his face. "I wish I could say something different." He seemed to have lost all hope.

"Tell me what to do," said Lord Campo, flopping into a chair. He shut his eyes and placed his hands on his forehead, very thoughtful.

Martina walked to the emissary. "You've done enough for our kingdom. Just inform the Council what happened." Then she said to the general, "Althar, you have a big task ahead of you."

The Chief of Army's eyebrows puckered in a frown. It looked like ten things came to his mind, but he could not guess an answer.

Lord Campo raised his gaze over his thick glasses.

The queen went on and instructed with a firm voice. "Only a powerful army can win wars. We must make our army bigger and stronger." Then she moved closer to the general and patting him on the shoulder, she concluded, "Althar, you're the commander of the new task."

General Althar nodded his agreement to the queen's request.

Quickly, Martina swept past a wood coat rack, grabbed her violet cloak, and wrapped it around her shoulders. "I must hurry. The war is not waiting for me, but peace is."

"Wait!" called Enzo, following Martina out of the Diamond Office. "Where are you going?"

"To see King Filippo!"

"You don't even know how to get there." Enzo shut the tall door of the room with a single pull of the handle. "I'm going with you!" he said loudly as he tried to catch up with Martina.

Queen Martina and Enzo soon left Diamond Palace. Crossing the west hills to Castella, they ran into Drago.

"I'm so glad that I found you," said Drago, pacing his gallop to stay next to Martina. "I heard what happened with Castella."

Martina pulled back on the reins, coming to a stop. "Yes, it's my duty to defend Brightalia. Our kingdom needs peace."

"Filippo is an enemy who will never surrender." Drago warned his sister. "Let me go with you. You'll need help."

Enzo kept trotting around the trees, waiting. "With us?" he asked with suspicion. Trusting Drago again took some serious effort. He was not too convinced it was a good idea. "Thank you, but … I think we can handle the business."

Martina remained silent. Her brain became a spinning top. She needed all the help she could get. But, could she believe in Drago again? She recalled Drago's eyes at her coronation. They revealed a different person, a healed heart. Martina looked into those eyes again. Then she said with a certain voice, "Let's move fast! We can't afford to waste another minute." White Diamond whinnied as she dug the spurs hard into her mare. The queen dashed ahead through the rocky way leading to Castella.

Drago and Enzo locked into a fast gallop determined to help the queen. They were running out of time.

The wind beat hard on their faces. The forest trees became so tall they resembled the towers at Diamond Palace. There in the deep jungle, the smell changed from fruity to putrid. The wild rustle of animals seemed to be chasing them. But with light or darkness, they never stopped until they reached their destination, Filippo's castle.

Queen Martina, Drago, and Enzo crossed the drawbridge. The front guards escorted them to the inner ground, an open area enclosed by the intimidating tall walls of the castle. Right there at the ward, King Filippo stood, waiting. He had been warned that Martina was on her way to his castle.

Filippo was not alone. A huge battalion of infantry stood behind him. They made perfect straight lines. They were armed to their teeth; swords, axes, maces, sickles, and daggers were among the many weapons. Long serious faces were the general consensus of the regiment.

Queen Martina swallowed a big lump that had formed in her throat. She could not avoid wondering if they would make it out of there alive! She made her greatest effort to stay calm and drained all negative thoughts from her mind, something that was not easy. She walked gingerly to where Filippo was. Drago and Enzo stood a couple of feet behind Martina.

King Filippo raised one arm, and the front line soldiers pointed their weapons at the queen. "You've saved me a trip," he said with a nasty grin.

Martina did not know what was worse, to be standing there or to have faced a pack of ralthors at the beach. She felt like a prey, a tasty one. But she needed to be strong for her people. One last bold attempt to solve the long-lasting crisis and recover her kingdom was all she had. "Brightalia is a kingdom of peace. It's our kingdom, and you don't have any right to take it away. Leave our land," demanded the queen.

A mischievous smile crawled over Filippo's face. "Losers! Don't you see my army?" The king turned to glare at his huge military force and then back at Martina. "I'm a fighter for lands. I'm a conqueror of a new empire." He seemed to be enjoying the moment.

"And I'm a fighter for peace and a conqueror of justice," disagreed Martina. She held up her arms to summon her magical sand. "This war will cease today."

But Filippo reached out quickly and clasped Martina's hands in a tight grip. Immediately, the king ordered with a deep voice. "Arrest them!"

"You won't get away with this," snorted Drago. He put up some resistance to the soldiers who secured him.

"Withdraw your troops, Filippo," said the queen. "Brightalia belongs to us!" Martina felt a strong pull when a young sergeant tied her wrists together behind her back.

The soldiers forced their heads backward. The smell of blood was soon to arrive.

Enzo was the first in line who felt a sword too close to his neck. "There's no need to slaughter us," he said almost crying. All of a sudden, his birthmark lit up as though a match were burning a tinder rope.

An immediate hush fell.

A high-ranking officer, who was beside Enzo, took a look at him and fell to his knees. Then it was the young sergeant. Then another soldier. Then twenty more. To Filippo's shock, the entire army of Castella were on their knees. They all removed their kettle hats and bent their heads in a sign of respect.

King Filippo was the only one left standing. A whisper quickly reached his ear.

"Enzo carries the mask of a fish on his left cheek." It was the Chief Officer. He eyed at Enzo one more time. Then, he turned back to Filippo. "He is the royal son, thought to be murdered with his father." He explained in a slow mumble. The officer took a deep breath before he concluded, "He's your cousin and actual King of Castella."

Filippo laughed at the claim with insanity. "I'm the only King of Castella." He scowled at the officer. Then his eyes flicked to Enzo, and pointing a stiff finger at him, he warned, "You're not our king. You'll never be."

"Fish-face! King of Castella?" Drago was thunderstruck by the unexpected revelation.

Enzo's eyes enlarged like two fried eggs. "Are you talking to me? Enzo Latte? There must be a mistake." The poor fisher was stunned. Straightaway, the image of his sick mom lying on the cot rushed to his head. He recalled she tried to reveal a secret of some sort before she died. After a long time, he understood why she kept repeating he was a special boy. Enzo looked at the queen.

Martina still had her mouth open in surprise. "You're truly a special boy."

Right away, Filippo drew his sword with raw anger. "Stand up and kill them." He ordered his army with a frenetic voice. He clomped across the lines of soldiers, but they refused to move.

Not a single army man obeyed the king's order. Instead, the soldiers released the hands of the three prisoners.

At the lack of response, Filippo reached inside his pocket and quickly threw a handful of magical black powder at Martina. "You can do nothing," he said, narrowing his gray eyes at the queen.

Martina tried to protect her face with her hands, but small particles still penetrated her eyes. She squinted into the sudden change in her vision. "What are you doing?" Martina blinked several times. The magical powder had caused her to see triple.

Filippo was not going to stop there. The magical dust was just the start of his battle. He did not hesitate and rushed at Enzo. "Your reign ends now. Even if I have to do it myself!" shouted the king with fury. As Filippo was ready to swipe his sword and behead the true king of Castella, another blade got in his way.

"Not that fast!" Drago yelled back at Filippo. He pulled hard on Filippo's sword, forcing him to jump away from the scared fisher.

Enzo reeled backward, and a soldier scurried to catch him before he fell. But what hit the ground was Enzo's jaw when he finally took a gander at his audacious defender – the last person who would have crossed his mind.

Filippo swayed to the side from the leap, but he managed to keep his balance. Then he launched himself at Drago with a quick blow of his sword.

Drago and Filippo engaged in a dangerous fight. Everybody could hear the sharp sound of the blades hitting against each other.

Drago was quick. He avoided most of the attacks by dodging sideways. His Bladeking skills arose just in time to face his opponent. Drago swung his sword toward Filippo's face. But Filippo was a well-trained fighter. He parried the fatal strike.

Martina could not see clearly. She tried to focus on her target. She aimed her eyes' rays at Filippo's sword, attempting to wrest it from his hands. But she was way off. Not only did she miss the weapon, she almost hit a soldier who was lucky enough to hurl himself to the ground before he was caught by the violet light.

Filippo pursed his mouth in a conceited smirk. "Your sister can't save you. Today will be your last day." He clubbed Drago's blade down with a brisk swipe.

Martina tried to follow every aggressive move. She remembered when she was young and played as a referee during Bladeking games. She felt the same butterflies in her stomach. She wished she could help. This was a real battle.

Filippo's training paid off. His strength was superior. After long stressful minutes, he had gained control of the fight. It was plain and obvious that the battle was coming to its end. Filippo pushed the point of his sword straight at Drago's throat.

Drago was choking. "Brightalia doesn't deserve you," he said in a strangled voice. He could hardly breathe. His sword was getting heavier by the second. He could not send another thrust.

"Castella wins," said Filippo with hatred in his eyes. The moment that he was waiting for finally came. Filippo raised his blade and lunged straight at Drago, going for his winning hit.

To the surprise of everybody, an arrow shot from a distance. Filippo's eyes popped out. He turned his body sideway, but he could not escape the fast flying weapon. A cry of sharp pain. A dull thud. Filippo lay on the ground with the arrow piercing his chest. His hand opened, and the sword rolled slowly to the side.

"You'll only be the king over my dead body." Those were the last weak words of Filippo. The king gasped on one last breath of air and then collapsed.

All gazes propelled to the crossbow. It was in the hands of the same officer who had recognized Enzo as King of Castella. He had ended Filippo's life. Yet, he was not fast enough to prevent Filippo from hurting Drago.

Drago also lay on the floor. His arm was badly injured. He was nothing but pain. He tried, but he could not keep his eyes open. They closed by themselves.

Martina rushed to her brother. "Drago!" she cried. With her triple blurry vision, she struggled to check the deep wound. "Talk to me, please. Stay here." Tears filled her eyes and slipped down her face.

"He will," said Enzo who hurried next to Martina. His facial expression revealed concern. Drago took on a risky battle to save him, and now he was fighting for his own life. "You've won Drago. You can't leave us now." Enzo hastily loosened his neckerchief and tied it with a knot around Drago's arm. "This will help," hoped the villager, feeling the cold skin of Drago. He kept twisting and tightening the piece of cloth to compress the wounded limb.

Except for Martina and Enzo, there was total silence in the ward. The entire army stood, looking like dead armor.

Time traveled fast, and Drago was not responding. He was bathed in sweat from head to toe. Martina attempted to find his pulse, and it was hardly existent. She was losing her brother.

Suddenly, Martina stood. "Move out of the way," she ordered Enzo. Her eyes shone a radiant violet color. A frown of concentration. And the queen urgently summoned her magical eyes' powers. As straight as she could, Martina fired a stream of violet rays at Drago's arm. The neckerchief disappeared, and the injury became exposed. Flaring like a Bengal light, the wound slowly transformed into a long violet scar.

After a few more agonizing seconds, the blackness in Drago's eyes faded. His sight was a bit hazy, but Drago had come to life again. Martina's face glowed with happiness. She gave her brother a hug so tight that it almost cracked his ribs.

At the end, it was Enzo who had to rest his body on the floor. He was pale and queasy, but with relief.

A stunning ovation came from the crowd. The entire army of Castella shouted out in joy.

Word quickly spread that Brightalia was saved. The long battles were over. Queen Martina and King Enzo agreed they would help each other to rule both kingdoms. The best part was that everybody understood that magic was good after all.

Upon her return to Brightalia, Queen Martina heard the sound of musical instruments. She was a block away from Piano Plaza.

Martina dismounted her horse and walked toward the plaza. Drago and Enzo cheered wildly right beside her.

A silvery voice sang the tune of a wonderful song. One composed for the queen.

A surprise welcoming awaited Martina. Villagers packed the place ready to celebrate the start of a new prosperous era for the kingdom.

Hearing the lovely melody, Martina made it to the center of the plaza. Her face shone, and her violet eyes glittered with joy.

There were all her people, even the main servants from the palace – Dante, Bruno, cook Donato, Giorgina, and her adorable nanny Mercy. General Althar and Lord Campo sat on a bench.

Dr. Brizio smiled from a corner. After many centuries, he finally returned to Enna Valley, not as an eagle, but as the elderly man he was.

A young girl fought her way through the crowd and brought the queen a bouquet of flowers.

"I can't ask for more!" Queen Martina gave the girl a warm hug. Looking at the sky and twirling in delight, Queen Martina raised her arms. A sprinkle of gleaming sand fell over the village. "Let's dance!" she said to the multitude.

Drago went to his sister. "I will always be here for you." He put his hands around Martina.

Behind them, Enzo moved in circles with vigor. His feet could not stay still.

Mercy tried to mimic the fancy gliding steps. She did her best, but only her chubby belly was in tune with the music.

Queen Martina turned around and easily copied the dance. She moved quickly and in a lively way. But it was Drago who concluded the dance. He hopped to the center and finished with a double spin. A new and funny posture that made all of them crack up with a laugh!

On Martina's bed, the old journal turned white, and the word "peace" became visible on the cover. The diary opened by itself to the last page, and the final magical words appeared:

Queen Martina never felt lonely again.
She was always surrounded by people who loved and cared about her.
For all the joy and peace Martina brought to her people,
She felt her dream was fulfilled.

Everybody started calling the island, Sandyland.
And as for Martina, she became known as the Sand Queen.

This is not the end of the book, but the beginning of the Sand Queen's life,
In this diary lives, the story of her magical eyes!

MEET THE ADVENTUROUS CHARACTERS

Princess Martina

Prince Drago

Enzo Latte

King Alessio

Queen Constanza

Mercy

Lord Campo

General Althar

Master Fabrizio

ACKNOWLEDGEMENTS

This book has taken me through an enjoyable learning journey; one that had a great partner. And I could not start any differently than thanking that person who read, reread, and then reread my story again. That best friend is my dear husband, Leonardo: kind, loving, outgoing, and at times, an innocent critic of my imaginary world that left my head spinning with new ideas. Since day one, he supported me when I showed him the first two pages of *Magical Eyes*. Thank you from the bottom of my heart.

Warm thanks to my three children. For asking the same encouraging question over and over again: When are you going to be done? For making me sprint away from the computer to pick them up or take them someplace. Or for patiently waiting for me to serve them dinner many evenings because I could not stop writing. It is only for them I did not finish the book in half the time. So glad I did. They are my life. They are my treasures.

Special thanks to the first professional eyes who read and edited my story, Cate Hogan. She taught me so much. For her smart feedback, her sound opinions, and her kind encouragement. And most of all, for challenging me to do more and better. Thank you a thousand times.

Finally, there is no way to end these lines without expressing my sincere gratitude to you, the passionate reader of this book. For being part of my magical adventure, I am so appreciative.

Never stop reading. Never stop dreaming!

ABOUT THE AUTHOR

Debut novelist Jessica D'Agostini has lived in Miami, Florida since 1990. Her love of magic and adventure drew her to children's books and pursuing a more creative life. Now, she spends hours glued to her computer meeting courageous characters, casting spells, and exploring fantasy worlds. She also enjoys traveling, reading, and walking the sandy beaches of South Florida with her husband and her adventurous crew of three children.

To learn more about Jessica D'Agostini, visit her website at
www.jessicadagostini.com